Seminary Ridge

Cemetery Ridge

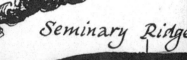

To Gettysburg ▶

The Battlefield of Gettysburg

July 1st, 2nd, and 3rd
1863

WE WERE THERE
At the **Battle**
of Gettysburg

WE WERE THERE
At the **Battle**
of Gettysburg

Alida Sims Malkus

Illustrated by
Leonard Vosburgh

Dover Publications
Garden City, New York

Bibliographical Note

This Dover edition, first published in 2013, is an unabridged republication of the work originally published in 1955 by Grosset & Dunlap, New York.

Library of Congress Cataloging-in-Publication Data

Malkus, Alida, 1895–

We were there at the Battle of Gettysburg / Alida Sims Malkus ; illustrated by Leonard Vosburgh.

p. cm.

"This Dover edition, first published in 2013, is an unabridged republication of the work originally published in 1955 by Grosset & Dunlap, New York."

Summary: Johnny and his sister find themselves caught between the Confederate and Union troops that converge in a small Pennsylvania town for a decisive Civil War Battle.

ISBN-13: 978-0-486-49261-2 (pbk.)

ISBN-10: 0-486-49261-3

1. Gettysburg, Battle of, Gettysburg, Pa., 1863—Juvenile fiction. [1. Gettysburg, Battle of, Gettysburg, Pa., 1863--Fiction. 2. United States—History—Civil War, 1861-1865—Fiction.] I. Vosburgh, Leonard, illustrator. II. Title.

PZ7.M294We 2013

[Fic]—dc23

2013019378

Manufactured in the United States of America
49261310   2022
www.doverpublications.com

The Author's thanks go to
MR. W. G. WEAVER,
*Burgess of Gettysburg and owner of
the Jennie Wade Museum,
for his cooperative aid.*

Contents

Illustrations

WE WERE THERE
At the **Battle
of Gettysburg**

CHAPTER ONE

Excitement in the Air

JONATHAN came quickly along the road to Gettysburg. He couldn't remember when the sun had been so hot, for the last day of June. He wished he was in the swimming hole. But he had to go to town.

Grandpa Blayne's farm was less than half a mile from Gettysburg, just north of the Chambersburg Turnpike. Johnny was halfway to town already. He wanted to run, but that would look as if he was scared.

Grandpa had said there was nothing to be afraid of yet. And Johnny wasn't afraid. Lots of boys of thirteen had seen battle. But General Early's Confederate soldiers had gone right through town four days ago, on their way to Harrisburg.

"Those Rebels didn't do a thing," Grandpa said.

No, they only cleaned out all the eggs, hams, beef, and flour they could lay their hands on. And some of the Confederate soldiers had lifted the hat right off the head of anyone they passed. Johnny had seen it himself.

But everything was so quiet and peaceful today. The fields and hills were never more green and blooming. The grain was ripening. So peaceful! And yet the Confederates had invaded Pennsylvania. But where were they? No one knew.

There was a strange excitement in the air. It seemed to tingle up from the road right through Johnny's bare feet. Near the edge of Gettysburg he began to run. He didn't stop until he stood panting in the shady street.

The afternoon sun poured down through the leafy roof and lay in golden pools on the dirt road. Two surreys came quickly down the street, headed out of town. The Joneses were packing up their wagon by the horse block.

The McDonnels were burying something in their back yard. Johnny ran on faster. Where Baltimore Street crossed the railroad he met the Wade boys.

"We're not a-leaving town," they said boldly. "We're a-staying."

Johnny's heart began to pound. It seemed to drum in his ears. What were the church bells tolling for? Were the Rebels coming back? Was the North going to let General Lee go right through Pennsylvania? Robert E. Lee had won 'most every battle so far, Grandpa said.

Johnny ran on. When he got to the store he stood still for a minute. A strange throbbing far away seemed to stir the air—it wasn't his ears either. Mr. Peebles stood behind the counter. He looked important and full of news.

"They're coming," he said. "The Union soldiers. Scouts came ahead. General Buford's on the way with four thousand cavalry."

"Could I get some coffee, Mr. Peebles, and the tobacco for Grandpa? And musket shot and—and five cents' worth of peppermint candy for Mary Lee?" Johnny asked quickly.

"Some folks are leaving town," Mr. Peebles put the coffee in the grinder, "but I aim to stay right here. Musket shot? Why, Johnny, the Confederates cleaned me out of that four days ago when

5

Early went through." The drumming sound was growing louder, coming closer. "You better get back to the farm, son, and tell your folks."

A crowd of townsfolk came swarming up into the store. "What's happening, Mr. Peebles?"

"Are the Rebs back?"

"Early cut the telegraph wires all along the line, so we can't get any news."

"Johnny Reb is near." Mr. Peebles' voice sank to a whisper. "A scouting party from Pettigrew's brigade was in town this morning—to get shoes. They went back to Cashtown when they found Buford was on the way with Union cavalry."

"And where's the Gettysburg Volunteers?"

cried the folks. "Most of our able-bodied boys are gone!"

"They went back," said Mr. Peebles, "to Harrisburg. What was left of 'em. George Sandow was the first one shot, picketing on the Baltimore Pike five days ago."

Johnny stood with eyes and ears glued to Mr. Peebles.

"Now you get off home, Johnny," the storekeeper said nervously, wiping his bald head with a red bandanna handkerchief. "You're right tall for your age, you look older. You might get taken for a drummer. Your folks wouldn't want to lose you like they lost your pa."

Johnny grabbed his packages and ran as if he'd been shot from a gun. The village was in a state of excitement. More folks were leaving, packing their wagons with valises and all kinds of things just stuffed in loose.

Old man Swanson had his parrot on his arm, and Grandma Jenks had her prize-laying hens on her lap. Old man Burns was closing his cobbler shop. He wore his best blue swallowtail coat with big brass buttons.

"Where'm I goin'? I'm goin' to volunteer with the Iron Brigade," he said.

The sun was dropping down the sky, and now Johnny could hear the pounding of horses' feet on the road, plain. They were right behind him. He never stopped running till he reached home. Grandma and Grandpa and Mary Lee sat at supper as he burst into the kitchen.

"Get your breath, son." Grandpa didn't seem surprised, but Grandma covered her head with her apron as Jonathan told the news.

Grandpa was used to war. He was over eighty years old, and he'd fought in Canada, and in the Battle of New Orleans later. His father had fought in the Revolution. Grandpa was tall and lean, with bushy black brows, and bristly gray mustaches and hair. Grandma was short, plump, curly-haired.

Grandpa got up now and hid his tobacco behind a brick in the chimney. "The Union can have anything we've got," he said, "but I'm going to take care of Grandma and you first, come what may."

"What is coming, Grandpa?" Mary Lee's blue eyes were dark with fear, and her pretty, dimpled face was pale.

*Grandpa hid his musket beneath a loose plank
in the floor*

A roll of drums on the still air, a distant bugle, was the answer.

"It's war, honey, war! And Gettysburg right in the middle of it." Grandpa took his musket down off the wall and hid it beneath a loose plank in the floor. "There's ruffians in the North as well as in the South," he said. "We might need this."

"Why will Gettysburg be right in the middle of it, Grandpa?" cried Mary Lee. Her eyes turned fearfully toward Johnny. He was always teasing her, but she adored him. Johnny had bolted a few mouthfuls of his supper and had run to the door to look up the road.

"Gettysburg is like the hub of a wagon wheel." Grandpa pointed with his pipe out over the fields. "Roads leading in to town from every direction, north, south, east, west. Hills to shoot from, woods to hide in—"

"They're coming!" shouted Johnny.

A cavalcade of horses burst from the town. It came thundering down the turnpike in a cloud of golden dust. The setting sun fell across the fields and never did the valley seem so lovely.

Down the road, two and three abreast, they

came—four thousand horse. They were passing the farm gate now, colors flying, horses neighing, scabbards clattering, hoofs pounding, officers singing out orders. You could smell the dust and the lathered horses.

"They're coming in," whispered Mary Lee.

An officer and two orderlies were riding up to the front door. It hadn't been opened all spring because the sun faded Grandma's carpet, but now they all rushed into the parlor and Grandpa opened the door.

The officer stood there; he saluted. "General Buford's command," he said. "We're making camp just beyond your farm, along the Chambersburg Pike. Could you let us take some chickens and eggs, perhaps hams too?" He was brisk, but smiling. "We'll pay you."

"No, sir, to both," said Grandma decidedly. "I don't want anyone scaring my chickens again. They know me and Mary Lee; we'll get the eggs. And you don't have to pay."

"Who's been scaring your chickens, ma'am?" the captain asked. "Has Early been through here?"

"General Early passed through four days ago,"

Grandpa told him. "He must be in Harrisburg by now." Grandpa led the way to the barn, Mary Lee and Johnny close at their heels.

The orderlies got potatoes, all the eggs that could be found, the whole batch of Grandma's fresh bread, and a gallon of buttermilk from the spring cellar under the kitchen.

"Our horses need grain and hay too," the captain said. Grandpa showed him what feed there was to spare. They stood for a while talking.

The wagons had all gone on, the captain said. Could the boy drive out with the hay first thing in the morning?

"There's no danger," the captain added. "The enemy's not in sight. There was a cavalry raid over east, and a scouting party turned tail this morning when they heard we were coming." He laughed. "Our forces are on the march," he added. "General Meade is in Taneytown—only nine miles south of here—and he plans to meet the enemy at Pipe Creek, not far from there. General Reynolds is camped down by Rock Creek, ready to join us in the morning.

"We have orders to find Lee. And we will!"

The captain laid a hand on Johnny's shoulder. "Don't worry, folks," he said. "From Hanover, Queentown, Manchester, Emmitsburg, the Union Army is on its way to Gettysburg."

"Maybe I'd best deliver the feed myself," said Grandpa.

"You'd better stay here, sir, in charge of your

house and farm," said the captain firmly. "This lad wants to help save the Union, don't you, son? And everything helps."

"Of course, sir," Johnny replied eagerly. " 'United we stand, divided we fall,' Grandpa always says. I'll be there at dawn." He went off to do his chores.

Dusk had fallen. Mary Lee went down to the root cellar. They'd need more vegetables to store in the spring cellar, just in case. She opened the door and as it swung to behind her, she lit her candle.

A scream rose in her throat, for among the turnips and potatoes a slave woman crouched.

CHAPTER TWO

In the Cupola

IT WAS not yet dawn, that fateful morning of July 1, 1863. Johnny and Grandpa Blayne went out to the barn to finish loading the big wagon with hay and feed for the cavalry horses.

"Jonathan," Grandpa said, "there is something in the air. There's going to be a big battle today. The South has its armies somewhere near. I can feel it." He shuddered.

"You know your pa was killed in the Texas border fighting, and your ma died of grief, mainly. You three were visiting her people in Virginny." Grandpa tossed the last forkful of hay up on the wagon, and Johnny spread it around.

"Well, let's have breakfast. The Rebels can't get here for another twenty-four hours anyway, I reckon." Grandpa harnessed and bridled old Sue.

"You know, son," he went on, "it's a shame to see them fighting like this over the Union, dividing the country, dividing families even. Lots of folks have both Southern and Northern blood in 'em—like you and Mary Lee. Your pa was a Yankee, your ma from Virginny. But it's the *U*-nited States that will keep us strong."

Back in the kitchen, Grandma had bacon and eggs and steaming coffee ready. Johnny ate quickly, stuffed two doughnuts in his pocket, and got up from the table.

"I wish I could go too," Mary Lee begged.

"You couldn't go; a girl?" Johnny snatched his hat off the deer horns by the door as he went. "Don't worry, Grandma," he called back. "I'll be home in an hour or so. You have the captain's word for it."

"It wouldn't be right for you to go, Mary Lee, honey," Grandma said. "Soon as it's light, run down to the root cellar for some turnips."

"I'll go now." And before Grandma could answer, Mary Lee was out the door.

The east was pink and the sun would soon be rising. Johnny drove out the gate and turned right on the Chambersburg Pike. As his eyes strained forward toward the cavalry camp, something stirred just behind him!

Out of the hay climbed Mary Lee and into the seat at his side. "I had to come, Johnny. I had to—there's something I have to tell you." She was brushing the hay out of her rumpled blond curls.

Johnny was furious. "I've a mind to turn back!" he exclaimed. "This is no place for a twelve-year-old girl!"

"Girls can help in wartime too. Listen, Johnny—"

But Johnny would not listen. He had seen a picket ahead and motioned her to be quiet. "Maybe they want us to keep still around here," he said. She was afraid to tell him about last night. He did not speak until the picket had passed them on and they were entering a small woods. A moment later a thud in the back of the wagon made them turn around—just in time to see a man slide out from under the hay and run off into the woods.

"How did he get there?" gasped Mary Lee. Thoughtful and troubled, they drove on into the camp, which lay between Oak Hill and Seminary

*They turned just in time to see a man slide out
from under the hay*

Ridge, about seven miles below Cashtown.

"He may have been a spy, or an escaped prisoner," Johnny said. "He must have hidden in the hay during the night. But what can we do?"

Mary Lee was frightened. She wanted to tell Johnny about the slave woman in the root cellar. But now she was afraid to. Surely *she* couldn't have been a spy. There was no time to think of it further for they were on the edge of the encampment. The camp was in a great bustle.

"Here, lend a hand, you boy," called a sergeant. "Fetch up some water from that little draw down there." Johnny had started to pitch out the hay, but he ran willingly to carry one, and then another, bucketful.

Two soldiers had finished pitching the hay out, the wagon was empty, and Jonathan climbed back into the seat.

"Wait, we need a boy," cried the sergeant. "The little girl can drive the wagon home, can't she? It's safe; we have pickets stationed all along the way.

"Here, soldier, you're replacing number-one picket. Take the little lady down that far; she'll be nearly home."

"Don't you need a drummer boy?" asked Johnny boldly.

"We might!" The sergeant grinned. "Here's your pail."

Johnny took the pail obediently, and when he returned Mary Lee was driving back down the road, big as life. The sun was rising, and by the

time she reached the picket line she'd be in sight of the farmhouse.

The cavalrymen were harnessing their horses, looking to stirrups and girths, filling canteens, wiping and loading guns. Johnny was kept carrying water until his arms were nearly pulled out of their sockets. It seemed as if he heard distant shots.

A cavalryman came galloping down the road. "The Rebels are coming down the turnpike," he cried. "Our scouts ran into their pickets, and were taken prisoner."

Suddenly, at a distant command, the cavalry were mounted and away, and the encampment emptied as if by magic. In a moment, gun carriages, guns, mules with guns strapped to their backs, lumbered after them. Horses and ambulances followed, with the rumble of wheels, the clank of metal.

It must have been going on nine o'clock. Johnny's arms ached from toting buckets. He sat down on a gun carriage and began to eat his doughnuts. Then, of a sudden, there was a great blast of cannon, and the sound of steady firing up along the Chambersburg Road.

Rat-tat-atat-tattat-tat, it never stopped, and now the boom of guns rolled down the road. Somewhere over west, Lee and his armies must be advancing. General Buford was to protect General Reynolds from the rear, the officer had said yesterday. But where was Reynolds?

"If I were up on the hill, near the Seminary," Johnny said to himself, "I could see all around, in every direction."

Maybe General Reynolds was somewhere over on the hill. Johnny could look up and see the cupola of the Lutheran Seminary rising above the trees on the top of the ridge. If he could get up into that cupola!

He made a dash across the turnpike and into the bushes at the foot of Seminary Hill. He stumbled and fell, and lay for a minute in the ditch beside the road. Right before his nose lay a pair of field glasses, dropped by some officer, no doubt.

What luck! He hung them around his neck and, stooping, ran in among the trees. It wasn't a steep slope, but he was out of breath by the time he came in sight of the Seminary. All the students had joined the Volunteers.

He could hear the noise of the fighting over west. People were rushing out of the big white buildings before him. Johnny crept around to the front door of the main building. Inside, he found his way to the spiral stairs that led up to the cupola.

No one saw him; he saw no one. He was trembling with excitement. He'd always wanted to climb up into the belfry and never had the chance.

Now, here he was! Up and up. At last the whole valley lay spread before him. There was Gettysburg opposite, to the east. There was his grandfather's farm, and the Chambersburg Pike running past it and leading away to the northwest, right by the foot of the hill.

"It's just like Grandpa said," he thought aloud. "The roads are just like the spokes of a wheel, and the town is the hub."

In between lay the wheat fields, the corn, the orchards, the farmhouses and barns. With his eyes tight to the field glasses the well-known scenes came close to him.

Almost at his feet lay the Millerstown Road, running southwest. And far away to his left also,

he could see where the Mummasburg Road led off
northwest. And the Carlisle Road, going due north
out of Gettysburg, straight as a surveyor's string.

There was a lot of movement south of town.
You couldn't rightly tell just what it was. And

soldiers were coming out of Gettysburg along the
turnpike! Reynolds' men!

Johnny ran from one window to the other. The
windows didn't open, but he could hear the rumble of guns on the west just the same. Smoke rose
up through the trees, in blue spirals and hundreds
of small, round puffs. Soldiers were coming along

the Chambersburg Pike down by Greenwood. Could they be Lee's men?

And someone was coming up the stairs! It might be the Confederates. No matter who it was, he mustn't be caught here. Where could he hide? Not a place! Yes, under the window seat; there was a panel loose. He worked it out and crawled under the seat, drawing the panel back in place just in time.

CHAPTER THREE

The Great Battle Begins

FOOTSTEPS and voices came closer. They were right beside him in the cupola.

"General Reynolds," Johnny heard one voice say, "I'm mighty glad you got here. My scouts ran into Lee's pickets early this morning. I stationed my cavalry at once on the hills on both sides of the road."

"I heard the firing," the other voice replied. "We were riding through Gettysburg. I rode on ahead of my men to meet you, Buford, and find out what it was."

"Look at that plain below, Reynolds," General Buford said. "An ideal place for a battle, closed in by hills and ridges."

"Right, and the field glasses show two mounds at the end of that ridge—natural fortifications."

"He means Round Top and Little Round Top," thought Johnny. He put his eye to a crack in the panel and saw a tall, dashing figure—General Reynolds.

"If we can take those hills," said the other general, "we can command the whole valley with our guns. It is a most suitable place. I'll send a messenger to General Meade at once, telling him that the enemy is advancing in large numbers and that we need help at once."

"A decisive battle should be fought here, rather than to fall back to Pipeclay Creek," Reynolds replied. He walked across the cupola. "The fighting looks heavy along this western slope," he said. "We must hold the Rebels back until General Meade can send reinforcements. I must get down there and join my men."

Johnny could see the two generals turn toward the stairs. All was quiet in the cupola. Johnny crept out and down the winding stairs. Fifteen minutes later he was scrambling down the slope toward the branch of Willoughby Run, the little stream at the foot of Seminary Hill.

He knew the place well, had gone fishing there

"A decisive battle should be fought here"

many a time. Buford's cavalry had tied their horses in the woods to the rear. They were spread out, to make it seem as though there were many more of them.

The patient mules, their small cannon strapped to their backs, waited behind the lines. Gun sites on the hoof, the mules could be moved quickly wherever needed. The sounds of battle came nearer.

Johnny ran forward. The fields sloped gently to the stream, and a number of rail fences wiggled along the meadows. In a little clearing, General Reynolds, mounted on his horse, was studying the battlefield. Suddenly—a whining, whistling zoom —the general fell forward on his horse, and slipped to the ground as his aides ran up.

"Shot right through the neck!" Johnny heard the cry.

He turned and ran wildly through the woods in the opposite direction. If he could only find a gun! A gun? What for? He didn't want to shoot anyone. He was a Yankee, but whom did he want to kill? His mother was a Virginian, wasn't she?

A swarm of soldiers came running through the

trees. They wore gray uniforms. They swept over him, caught him up. He was carried with them down the slope as they fled from the rain of bullets, and retreated across Willoughby Run.

The firing was ear-splitting. Buford's artillery kept a steady stream of fire from the breastworks up on the ridge. Johnny could see the mules plant their feet squarely to take the shock of the firing. Two of them fell dead.

The Rebel grays surged back up the slope and he with them. A shell exploded almost in his face and he fell flat. A soldier fell beside him. Johnny lifted him up, but the soldier died, right there in Johnny's arms. He was young, almost as young as Johnny himself, and he wore a gray uniform.

After that there was only one thing to do. He could fetch water from the Run for anyone who needed it. Sometimes he bathed their faces, gave them water to drink. And he tied up wounds, too.

The tide of battle swept back and forth. The Confederates came on with such force that the boys in blue were swept right out of their position and pushed up behind the granite ridges of Seminary Hill. The Rebels charged with such fury right into the Northern ranks that hundreds of them were taken prisoner.

The slopes were covered with the dead and wounded. Guns, knapsacks, canteens strewed the meadows. Groans pierced the frightful din.

"Give me some water, boy."

"Thank you, thank you, son!"

Stretcher bearers came through the woods. They were carrying the wounded back across the Chambersburg Road. A soldier fell at Johnny's feet, another Confederate. He was in tatters and he wore no shoes. He had been shot in the leg.

Johnny tore off his pants leg and used it to tie a tight tourniquet. The soldier was not much taller than Johnny himself, and he couldn't be more than sixteen.

"Help me," he moaned. "I promised Ma . . . they burned our home to the ground. . . ."

Johnny pulled the boy's arm over his shoulders and put an arm around him. He tried to lead him in the direction where the stretcher bearers were going. But the young soldier had fainted.

A cavalry horse picketed near was circling round

its blue-uniformed rider, stretched on the ground. The soldier was dead. Johnny untied the horse and led it over to the Southern soldier boy. He threw water in the boy's face from a canteen he'd picked up. When the boy came to, Johnny helped him up into the saddle. They got across the road somehow, through a rain of bullets and exploding shells.

Up in the woods there was an old stone mill. The Rebels had made it into a hospital, and near by were a number of tents. An ambulance and some horses stood close by.

An orderly helped Johnny lift the wounded soldier down from the horse, and tied it near by. "You belong to Heth's division, bub?" he asked.

"No place for you, boy," said another. "But here, fetch me a bucket of water, quick!"

"Here, lend a hand, son."

And so it went. Johnny got so he could see the surgeon work on the wounded and not be sick at his stomach. He fetched and carried, and held water to dry lips. And it was all the same whether the wounded soldier wore the blue or the gray.

But it was all a terrible dream, a nightmare. Time passed. *He must get back.* "What will Grandma think? I promised her yesterday. . . . Yesterday?" he cried aloud.

Why, it was only today. Years had gone by since this morning. Yet it was barely two o'clock now by the sun. He sat for a while with his back to a tree.

The horse he had found still stood tied to a post. He led it down to the mill stream and they both drank. Then he mounted and started through the woods.

Shells were bursting in the air along Seminary Ridge. A small company came riding out of the woods directly in front of him. Johnny saw a handsome officer, with white hair and small beard. He was in spotless uniform. He sat his gray horse superbly, and trotted rapidly ahead of his aides.

"There's General Lee!" cried a soldier, spurring past Johnny. "He's going down to the Seminary. The fighting's not over. The battle's spread east and north of Gettysburg."

Johnny dug his heels into the horse's flanks and followed down the road after General Robert E. Lee. The sounds of battle reached them on the wind. The general galloped swiftly on, and out of sight.

Johnny's horse went slower and slower. He could not keep up. "More fighting! I must get home." Now he had time to be scared. What had happened to Mary Lee and Grandma and Grandpa? The boom of cannonading grew louder.

"Gittiup, gittiup, old boy," Johnny urged the horse along. He slapped the reins across its flanks, and pulled on the bit. The cavalry horse shot for-

He sat his gray horse superbly

ward, lickety-split, down the road to Gettysburg.

"Halt!" Two bayonets were crossed in front of his horse. "You can't pass here. What you doing on this here road?" A Confederate sentry looked up along the barrel of his gun.

"I—I'm just trying to get back home," Johnny stammered.

"Oh, you are, are you, you little Northern spy! Get off that horse. It belongs to this outfit." The sentry jerked Johnny down and pushed him across the road and inside a high fence. There was a log cabin there, not far from the MacPhersons' barn. The soldier pushed Johnny through a door before which a sentry stood.

"Now get outta those clothes," said his captor. "The shoes, too." The Rebel's feet were small and Johnny's were large for his age.

The Rebel kept his gun pointed at him, so there was no use in Johnny's refusing. The young Confederate stripped him of his blue cotton shirt, his blue jeans, and his good new boots.

Johnny felt thoroughly wretched. "I have to have some clothes," he protested. "I can't go around this way."

"That's right, sho' nuff, you cain't," grinned the young picket. "So you'll just stay right here." He disappeared with Johnny's clothes, backing out the door with his gun pointed at his naked prisoner.

CHAPTER FOUR

A Yankee Prisoner

HOW was he to get out of here? How, how was he to get his clothes back? Johnny looked desperately around the little cabin. It was a sturdy log lean-to, and, by giminy, there was a loft in it. Looked like a square manhole between the ceiling beams, and a trap door.

But it was away over his head. He couldn't possibly get up there. Now Johnny's anger rose to sudden fury. He had to get some clothes and he wasn't going to get shot to get them!

That little Johnny Reb thought he was a spy, did he? All right, he'd be a spy! He'd find out what was going on, and he'd get out of this and back to the farm.

"There's got to be a way!" he cried aloud.

An old fence rail lay along the wall. He picked it

up and in his rage he gave a tremendous push at the trap door to see if it would give. It stuck tight. Maybe it was nailed in. He gave another desperate push, with all his might.

It lifted up. But at this moment the noise of horses outside, and voices, made him cower down out of sight of the one little window. People were going into the adjoining building. He could hear the tramp of feet, and wood scraping against wood. After a while he stood up and pushed again at the trap door.

It might be just a blind attic, but there was a ray of light up there; he'd try it. This time he pushed the lid clear up. With a thumping heart he propped the rail against the opening and began to shinny up. Would that old rail hold him?

It started to split. With a desperate reach for the edge of the opening, he hitched upward and caught hold just as the rail cracked and fell to the floor. He drew himself up into the loft and quickly replaced the lid.

He sat motionless for a moment, hugging his knees. Now he could hear the voices very clearly.

The loft over the lean-to opened into another loft. He crawled through and found that the light he had noticed came from a small window.

Someone had slept up here. There was a pallet on the floor and a dirty blanket, and nothing more. Yes, there must be, there was, another trap door,

close over against the wall. He put his eye to a crack and looked down. They were carrying in wounded soldiers below. Orderlies were laying fresh straw on the floors, a surgeon was already at work.

"Cheer up, my brave fellows," the surgeon was

saying. "You won the day. The fighting was heavy, and for a time Reynolds' regiments were ahead; but we pushed them back—with a great loss to them."

"If we had only had our cavalry," gasped a soldier whose arm was tightly bound. "The Yankees got reinforcements, just when we had them licked."

"We're getting fresh troops too," the doctor said. "Leave it to General Lee. Ewell came down by the road from the North; Heth and Rodes are on their way."

Johnny felt suddenly guilty. He was eavesdropping. He guessed he could never be a spy. There was going to be more fighting and it frightened him.

The doctor and attendants were very busy with the wounded now. The boom of guns had never stopped, and now a fearful blast shook the cabin. It grew terribly hot in the loft and the window would not budge.

Down below they were bringing in more wounded. The groans and gasps hurt to hear. Johnny put his eyes to a crack. He could see a soldier in blue; a Union soldier. He lay right beneath Johnny.

"Hist," the man was saying to the orderly. "I'm not a Yank. I'm a Confederate; a spy."

"Well, naow, ain't that just fine!" grinned the orderly.

"I've got to see General Lee. Take me to him."

"You're no spy! And you cain't see Lee." The man would not believe him.

"Then let someone carry my message to him. Say it's Harrison." The orderly was afraid not to do so, and went out. He was back in a few minutes with a young lieutenant.

"Harrison!" exclaimed the officer. "You here! What happened? And did you find out where General Stuart is? General Lee is very much upset at not hearing from him. We need the cavalry badly."

"Not so fast." Harrison tried to sit up but fell back. "I like to be sure. The general sent for me three days ago, back at the Chambersburg Pike headquarters. I told him then that the Army of the Potomac had crossed the river, and that Meade was already on his way to Taneytown. Was I right?"

"Harrison, you're one of the few scouts whom the general has any confidence in. Why, on the strength of what you told him he called back all his Corps officers to gather here.

"But the cavalry? We have no cavalry here. And the General relies on Stuart for news of the enemy too."

"When I left General Lee the night of June

twenty-eighth, I made my way to Gettysburg. I disguised myself as a Negro mammy escaping to friends in Harrisburg. Then I learned that Gen-

eral Early had gone through Gettysburg to Harrisburg only four days before.

"Stuart? Curse this foot!" the scout groaned. "Stuart crossed the Potomac at Seneca, shortly after Lee had crossed. Stuart cut the telegraph lines at Rockville, and tore up the railroads. Knowing his ways, I figured he'd move fast."

"Where did he go?" asked the lieutenant eagerly. Up above them, Johnny pressed his ear to the crack in the floor.

"He went almost straight north, toward Carlisle. Following Lee's orders, he was to meet General Ewell there. He kept east of the Federal lines all the way. A man from Hanover said Stuart had passed that way several days before. So he must have got to Carlisle yesterday. I sent word to him to ride night and day to Gettysburg."

Johnny hardly dared breathe. He was frightened. Was this the man who had stolen a ride in Grandpa's hay wagon this very morning? If so, he certainly wasn't disguised as a Negro mammy then.

"When Buford came into Gettysburg yesterday, I followed his men into the store. I listened. They spied me, but I got away from 'em, and out to a farm just outside town. I hid in a barn, in the hay-loft. I was afraid I'd be discovered when the hay was pitched down. So I hid in a root cellar. Later I took off my woman's clothes and face stain; I had on a Union uniform underneath. I hid in the back of a hay wagon, and got a ride into Buford's camp this morning."

"What did you find out?" asked the lieutenant.

"I found out the number of Union troops and where they're stationed. And that they've been all ordered here. Tell General Lee," Harrison grasped the lieutenant's arm urgently, "tell him that there'll be ninety thousand Union men here. Get that, Lieutenant? Ninety thousand by tomorrow."

"You're sure, Harrison?" The lieutenant jumped to his feet.

"I'm sure. I heard Buford send word to Meade this morning. I'm as sure of it as I am that the South either has got to strike quick, right away, or else retreat."

The lieutenant didn't wait to hear the scout's opinion. He had already gone. A moment later both the orderly and the volunteer helpers hurried out to meet more sorely wounded men. There was

47

Here was Johnny's chance

no more room on the floor of the log cabin.

Here was Johnny's chance. Quick as thought, he pulled the blanket around him, opened the trap door, and let himself down the ladder. Harrison had turned his face away, and none of the wounded paid any attention to him. They were too sick to care.

From the loft Johnny had noticed some gray uniforms piled in a corner—the stained and tattered clothing taken from the wounded. He snatched up a shirt and was about to slip it on when he heard someone returning.

He lay down quickly against the wall and, naked as he was, pulled the old blanket over himself. It was a woman! A farmer's wife, a volunteer nurse. She went from one to another and came to Johnny.

"What ails you, son?" she asked kindly. She took hold of the blanket to draw it back.

"Nothing, nothing, ma'am," he stammered, clutching at the blanket. "I—I was just stunned, I guess. They took my clothes away, and I found this old blanket. And—and I want to get out of here. I'm all right."

"Well, you seem all right," the woman said. "If you're sure you weren't hit and don't hurt no place, I guess you can go.

"Maybe you'd better have some clothes. Are these yours?" She handed him a shirt and trousers, patted him on the shoulder, and went on.

Dressed in the battle-stained gray, cuffs and trousers turned up, and a pair of worn-out shoes on his feet, Johnny hurried outside.

"Me, in a Southern uniform!" he thought. Suddenly he remembered the field glasses. Gone! He didn't even know when he had lost them. What a shame!

But he didn't need glasses to see that the road home was cut off. It was under a steady stream of bullets and exploding shells. The noise of battle never stopped.

Johnny walked quickly along, as though on some errand. And now happened the most remarkable thing of this tremendous day.

Out of a cook tent came a camp cook, an orderly, who handed Johnny a tray, and said, "Boy, take this up to General Lee. Up in that little house above the road."

CHAPTER FIVE

The Trembling Earth

THE tray had three glasses of buttermilk on it. When he had delivered it, Johnny thought, perhaps he might escape. But as a prisoner, what chance would he have of getting back home?

He walked carefully up the hill. It was old Mary Marshall's house he'd been sent to. He stopped before the door.

"Come in, come in, boy." It was General Lee himself. "Well, what a young Rebel we have here!" He laughed and laid a hand on Johnny's shoulder, as he stepped into the parlor and put the tray down on a table.

"Now tell me," the general went on, turning to one of the officers with him. "General Hill, when you advanced from Willoughby Run, you say you placed your artillery on both sides of Oak Hill opposite us?"

"Yes, General," Hill replied. "That was about one o'clock. And as late as eleven-thirty the enemy had held Gettysburg, and all of Seminary Ridge up to Oak Hill. And their General Howard had set up headquarters and a reserve artillery on Cemetery Hill." General Hill looked pale and tired.

"The Federal troops were stationed north of the town then, too?" asked Lee, seating himself at a table on which a map was spread.

"They were, General. But there was a wide gap in their line. And the Yankees fought with unusual determination. My troops moved forward; and just as the battle seemed to be going against us, General Ewell came down the Carlisle Road from the north, and shortly afterward Rodes' division closed in on the west. So we had a solid line of the Gray."

"Perfect! It could not have been more perfect if it were planned!" exclaimed General Lee, nodding.

"And so, sir," one of Lee's aides put in eagerly, "when our General Early came marching down the York Road from the east—well, sir, we had the enemy surrounded on three sides, with his back to Gettysburg."

"I did not want to have a major battle here," said General Lee, shaking his head.

"But the enemy surprised us, sir," replied the young officer. "General Hill had to give battle, first at Willoughby Run, then here. For the last two hours the fighting has been terrible."

"The men must be exhausted," said Lee.

"We lost heavily this morning," nodded his aide. "An entire brigade was captured."

"But by the time I arrived, some fifteen minutes ago," said the general, rising from the chair where he had been sitting, "the enemy had been pushed back right off this ridge. Buford is still falling back to the southwest. And we are closing in on the town. Come, I must watch this from the ridge." The general hurried out, and his glass of buttermilk stood untouched on the table.

From the door Johnny saw him mount his beloved gray horse, Traveller, and disappear up Seminary Hill. Johnny stood bewildered. What should he do now?

"There's going to be still another terrible battle," he thought. He threw his arm up before his eyes as if to ward it off.

"What's the matter, son?" a hand touched his shoulder. "Not scared? Course not. Here, take my horse and follow after the general, quick! Give him this note."

First thing he knew, Johnny was galloping off on a good horse. What else could he do, under Rebel guns? If he could only get down to the foot of the ridge, below the Seminary, it wouldn't be more than half a mile straight across to the farm.

General Lee was talking to a burly officer with a dark, heavy beard. Johnny slipped off the horse and respectfully presented the note. The general took it, smiling his thanks, and Johnny could not help liking him.

"General Longstreet, it's from you," laughed Lee. "But you got here first."

They were standing on the crest of a granite ridge. Below them they saw that the Northern army had been pushed back almost into town, from the northeast. And northwest of town, Ewell was driving them back over the Chambersburg

Pike. Johnny, waiting for further orders, could see clearly from where he stood close to the generals.

"I've just sent word to Ewell," said General Lee, "to push through Gettysburg and take Cemetery Ridge, if he can." He pointed to where the ridge rose south of the town.

"General, I don't think we should go ahead," said Longstreet impatiently. "I think we should fall back and cut the Northern army off from the road back to Baltimore and Washington."

"Longstreet," replied Lee calmly, "if the enemy is there, we must attack him. If we do not fight him, he will fight us. Our men, in spite of this morning's losses, are excited with victory. We are better clothed and fed than ever before."

"It is not a good plan, General," argued Longstreet sharply. "The Yankees have already taken over Cemetery Hill in great numbers. An attack now would be dangerous—we can't be sure of success."

Johnny thought General Longstreet acted angry. "My battalions have not all come up," he said stubbornly. "Pickett's at Chambersburg, Hood is guarding the rear."

"Now, General, look!" Lee spoke quietly. "We're sweeping down toward Gettysburg. We'll take the town."

At this moment a horse came dashing up. "Lieutenant Smith reporting, sir." The rider saluted. "General Ewell doubts that he can take Cemetery Hill without some support on his right."

"Lieutenant," replied Lee quietly, "you will have to tell the general that we have no supporting troops to send him. But while the enemy is on the run is the time to pursue him. Look, Longstreet!" He pointed across the valley. The long gray line was swarming down. And from the south the Blue-coats could be seen pouring out of the town.

The Rebels were taking Gettysburg!

Johnny could not bear it. He could wait to see and hear no more. He slipped behind a bush, no one was paying any attention to him, and began to scramble down Seminary Ridge.

The thunder of approaching battle was deafening. Shells were exploding like puffs of cotton over the fields. Bullets whizzed and whined overhead. One almost took Johnny's ear off; it stung his cheek.

A hundred yards away, the boys in blue were running and stumbling down the fields, turning to shoot as they ran.

Only half a mile to town! Half a mile of death and destruction. But he must make it. He ran out onto the field, crouching low, dodging. Only a little way to the farm. Grandma, Mary Lee, Grandpa!

"Are you there?" he cried out to them silently.

The earth was spouting and exploding all around him. He ducked and zigzagged and ran and ran. With a terrible noise two flaming balls struck together in mid-air before his very eyes. The earth seemed to tremble beneath him.

The explosion threw him to the ground. He lay stunned, his face in a furrow, while the fury passed over him. His sobs were smothered in the warm dirt.

Something caught him up by the collar, pulled him to his feet, wiped the earth off his face. "Scared, son?" A smiling face looked down into his. A tall, lean Southerner had his arm around him.

"Thought for a minute y'all was daid. Mighta been trompled on, son. Wa'al, you're all right, I see. . . ." His words could not be heard above the yells and the screaming of cannon balls.

Then for a moment the tide of battle seemed to stand still. For a moment Johnny stood there, steadied by the Rebel soldier. It seemed to Johnny as if something bright shone in the midst of the battlefield, the field once bright with wheat.

"I'll see you safe into taown." The soldier's

Johnny stood there, steadied by the Rebel soldier

voice rose for a moment above the fearful din. Then the battalions of the South swept on, carrying Johnny and the soldier with them.

They struck the turnpike, crossed it. Johnny was running along as though carried by a great wind. The Southern attack had ended in the rout of all the Northern army that had come out to find the Rebels that day.

The roar of victory rose over the shooting. The yells of the Rebels were added to the stampeding of thousands and thousands of feet.

"We've taken Gettysburg!"

"The Yanks are all prisoners!"

CHAPTER SIX

Night Falls on Gettysburg

OVER the road, through a fence. It was his grandfather's west fence and it lay flat. Across the pasture, right up to his very door, Jonathan Blayne was swept in the Confederate advance.

He clung to the kitchen porch as the foot soldiers rolled on into Gettysburg; and there he lay. The door opened.

"Poor boy! They took no heed of him. Just let him lie, those Rebels, and one of their own, too."

It was Grandma. Johnny raised his head as she stooped to lift him up. "Grandma, it's me! Don't you know me?"

"Johnny, Jonathan! In a Confederate uniform! Oh, Johnny, you haven't joined the Rebels?" Grandma gathered him into her arms, weeping.

The battle passed on like a great wave. The fields were destroyed, the house and barn riddled with shot. Johnny could hear the chickens screeching and cackling, the cows lowing with fear. Beyond them the fields were smoking, and they could see the glint of cannon north of the village.

"Where's Grandpa and Mary Lee?" Johnny asked Grandma.

"Mary Lee's down in the spring cellar. I hid her. Grandpa went off to town before the fighting moved this way. He carried in some provisions for our boys. They're up on Cemetery Ridge. Oh me, oh my!''

Grandma covered her head with her apron and said in a muffled voice, "We thought maybe you were killed in the fighting. We could hear the guns all day, even from over the other side of the Seminary. What a day!"

Johnny looked at her dumbly. Huh, what a day!

"I'm hungry, Grandma," he said. "Don't cry."

While she was preparing his food, Mary Lee came up the cellar stairs. "Oh, Johnny," she cried. "It's all my fault. I—I fed a spy—last night—she —he was in the root cellar." Mary Lee burst into tears.

"She?" Johnny asked dimly. Last night was so long ago.

Mary Lee explained, while Johnny drank his milk and ate the scrambled eggs and fresh bread. "And when I went to hunt eggs in the loft this morning, I found the mammy clothes. So it *was* the man—"

"I know," Johnny nodded. "But this battle was bound to happen anyway, Mary Lee. You ain't to blame for it." Suddenly he felt very weary. "I'll tell—all about—tomorrow." His head dropped on the table. He was asleep.

They managed to get him into the back bedroom, and he lay where he dropped. Grandma didn't even try to take the Confederate uniform off him.

Dark fell, and after the thundering noise of the day the quiet was beautiful. Even a few crickets chirped in the meadow. Grandma left a light in the window for Grandpa. The hours passed and he did not come.

The old clock struck midnight at last. Still Grandpa did not come. It was four in the morning when Grandma heard old Sue's trot-trot turning into the gate. Grandpa didn't wait to put her up for the night, but hurried in.

"Ma, you and Mary Lee all right? And Johnny?"

"He's back, Pa. Came in a couple hours after you left. Oh, where were you? It was terrible here."

"I wouldn't have gone, Ma, if I could have guessed our boys wouldn't hold out. Nobody thought the Rebs could break through our lines, much less get into town." Grandpa Blayne was in a fighting mood.

Grandpa Blayne was in a fighting mood

"Lee himself is down in town, talking with his generals. Most folk have cleared out. The Rebs took five thousand prisoners, and as many are dead or wounded. None of the townsfolk hurt, though." He sank into a chair disconsolately.

"It was a rout," he said. "Our troops ran like rabbits, with the Rebs at their heels. They hid in yards and cellars, anywhere. The town is littered with stuff. They threw away their arms, and the Rebs captured 'em by hundreds.

"They just lifted up their hands, Ma," he said bitterly. "I saw it all from old man Burns's house. He fought with the Pennsylvania Volunteers this morning. He was wounded, but came back, with the Iron Brigade. By gum, he was wounded again, and still went back. Just a scratch, he said. Ma, he's not much younger than me; he's seventy-three."

"And you're eighty-three, Pa—too old to have to fight."

"Well, John Burns is the only civilian in Gettysburg who's fighting. But the town hasn't anything to be ashamed of. It already gave its quota to the army, and the Volunteers held their own. And the townsfolk hid what was left of Reynolds' corps, fed 'em and nursed 'em.

"The South didn't lose as many dead or prisoners as we; but they lost plenty. I hear Lee says he'll have eighty thousand men as soon as Stuart and his cavalry get here, and General Pickett's two brigades are coming in from Chambersburg."

"Then—then the fighting's not over?" Grandma asked.

"Ma, you might as well know—Lee gave orders to commence battle first thing in the morning. They say that he said, 'If we don't whip them, they will whip us.'"

"What will ever become of us?"

"Don't give up, Ma. It's not so bad. The South has made a great mistake." Grandpa lowered his voice. "They should have gone on while they had the Union soldiers on the run, and they should have taken Cemetery Ridge. Early yesterday morning General Howard took over the Ridge for a retreat. And the first ranks of the retreat last evening got back up there."

"Have we many up there now?" Grandma asked.

"All afternoon, and ever since dark, they've been

pouring in there." Grandpa waved his arms. "Men, guns, mules, ammunition. Sime Hayes and I drove out early. Our boys are working and sweating, dragging up cannon over those boulders, building up breastworks.

"Right in the middle of the rout General Hancock came galloping up on a big black horse. He's a wonder. He took charge and put heart in the men. He's got General Wadsworth on Culp's Hill, and Geary came in by the Emmitsburg Road before I left."

"But General Meade, he's in command. Where is he?" Grandma asked.

"He got in about one o'clock, had to come from Taneytown. Oh, the North ain't going to take this lying down. We got the Union to fight for; that means the strength of the whole country. And freedom for slaves, too." Grandpa struck his fist into his palm.

"We'll win! There'll be something like ninety thousand troops when they all get together here. The Ridge is bristling with guns. They're back of the stone walls, and even back of the tombstones.

"First thing after sunup we'll have to go into town and help care for the wounded. The borough is filled with the dead and dying. The churches are taking in the wounded. But they haven't enough hands."

"This will be the last night's sleep for many," Grandma said sadly. "God help them—and us." Her hands trembled as she turned down the lamp.

CHAPTER SEVEN

The Little Nurse

A STRANGELY quiet morning dawned, on this July 2, 1863. No booming guns, no battle shouts, no clouds of smoke disturbed the sultry silence. But the scent of gunpowder still hung over the valley.

Mary Lee, Grandma, and Grandpa Blayne sat at breakfast. It was a hearty one, fried potatoes, apples, eggs, and toast.

"Can't tell what we'll have left to eat after today," Grandma said. "Mebbe we'd best wake Johnny now. Who can tell what will happen this day?"

"It was awful yesterday, Grandpa." Mary Lee shuddered. "The shooting was so bad over by Rock Creek, you could not see for smoke. The house shook. And Grandma's blue vase just fell off the shelf and cracked. The chickens, poor things—"

"Oh, war, oh, war!" But Grandma did not throw her apron over her head today. Her jaw was firm. "Ain't no use wringing our hands. We can say our prayers and do our best."

"Let's get that Rebel uniform off the boy." Grandpa got up and went off to call Johnny.

Johnny came to the table with his old clothes on. He ate as if he had not eaten for a week, and as if he might not eat again for another week. He tried to tell them what had happened to him yesterday.

"I heard them say that General Lee had ordered there was to be no thieving, and no destruction of property. He said they should not repay evil for evil. That was pretty straight of him, wasn't it, Grandpa?"

"No damage to property, only to people," said Grandma sadly.

"Troops don't pay much attention to such orders, I'm afraid," Grandpa said. "We've treated the South pretty bad sometimes ourselves."

"You know what General Early asked from the

town of York, Grandpa, with only seven thousand people?" said Johnny. "I heard about it last week. He wanted a hundred and sixty-five barrels of flour, thirty-two thousand pounds of beef, two thousand pairs of boots, *and* a hundred thousand dollars in cash money! Of course they didn't have it!"

Grandpa nodded absent-mindedly. He ate quickly and went out into the misty dawning to see the damage done the day before. "Don't you come out, Ma," he said.

He came back with a haversack, two canteens, two field glasses, picked up on his own land.

"It looks as though twenty thousand buffalo had stampeded over the place," he said grimly. "Most of the sheep and chickens are dead. I don't know what happened to Kitzmiller, and Kreagy, and Crawford, up the road. Their farms are still smoking. Stretcher bearers are still taking the wounded off north, to the Alms House, I guess, and some field hospitals. Let's see how Johnny Reb is fed." He opened the haversack.

"Hmm, moldy corn bread and some sowbelly. No wonder they throw it away!"

"We'd better be getting in to town, Pa." Grandma was bustling around. "While you and Johnny do what you can for the stock—"

Johnny and Mary Lee came rushing in to the kitchen. "Oh, it's terrible outside! The fields between here and Rock Creek are covered with guns and dead horses—and soldiers."

"Mary Lee," Grandpa was putting together all their household medicines and salves, and Grandma was tearing up old sheets, "you go up in

the attic, honey, and look out the window to see if there's a white flag flying just outside town. Sime Hayes said he'd fly one if we're needed there, half-mast if we should stay here."

A moment later Mary Lee's voice shrilled down from the attic. "It's there, Grandpa, the signal for us to come! And the roof is full of holes up here."

In ten minutes they were on their way into town, with a few extra clothes, all their sheets, a few treasures in Grandma's old carpetbag—the rest were hidden in the stone-walled spring cellar. Old Sue was hitched with the two-year-old filly.

It was barely six o'clock, but already heat lay over the valley.

"It'll be safer in town," Grandpa shouted over the clatter of wagon wheels on the gravelly road.

Some sudden shooting tore the quiet air and the horses bolted clear into town. The neat little village of Gettysburg had been trampled by two great armies. They had swept like a hurricane through the streets.

The lanes were cluttered with army equipment. Fences and gardens were down. Doors and windows stood open, houses left unguarded had served both North and South for a night. And many still slept, the long last sleep, where they fell.

Grandpa turned quickly down a lane toward Sime's house. They hadn't seen a single sentry.

Sime Hayes was a thin little man with a high, squeaky voice. "They ain't gone," he cried. "But the fightin's all moved south, so they're patrollin' south o' Central Avenoo and the railroad tracks. The Rebs took off all the prisoners who could walk," he said as he helped them unload the wagon, "but there's plenty left. You're needed."

He led the way next door. "The Joneses cleared out early yesterday," he explained, "and some men were brought in here. Handier than the churches or the schools. Ma's looking after these boys. You and Mary Lee can spell her; she's awful heavy on her feet."

Mrs. Hayes surely was heavy—over two hundred pounds. She was panting. She'd fed escaping Union soldiers all night. Some hadn't eaten for twenty-four hours. Now she collapsed and Sime took her home.

"Come on, children, we'll take care of this." Grandma tied on her apron.

The house was full of soldiers, both the gray and the blue. They lay on the beds and the floor.

"Let's get these boys on pallets, Ma," said Grandpa Blayne at once.

"You tear me up the sheets we brought, Mary Lee, honey." Grandma had rolled up her sleeves and taken over. "Johnny, you fetch water in from the pump and make up a fire in the kitchen stove. We'll need hot water."

Johnny came back in and helped get the soldiers on pallets. "You can wash their hands and faces and comb their hair, Mary Lee," Grandma said. "Make 'em as clean and comfortable as possible."

Mary Lee brought a basin of fresh water, with a sponge and towels, and gently and carefully she washed the grimy faces and hands. Each man had a fresh towel and clean warm water.

"Ma'am," gasped a soldier in blue whose eyes glinted feverishly. "I haven't had a bath—well, this is Heaven. You've no idea what we came through to get here. Marched thirty-two miles from eight in the morning till nine that night, three days ago. Second Corps Infantry; no corps ever beat that record in this war."

"Now you lie still, son," Grandma said

"Now you lie still, son. I'm going to send Johnny for the doctor," Grandma said.

"The Iron Brigade, that's what they call us."

"Aw, you don't know nothin', brother," grinned a boy in gray. "We slept in the rain for a week, then went another week without any water. My shoes was so bad I couldn't wear 'em. So I wore my feet instead. Wore 'em plum out. Look, Ma! Can you clean 'em up and bind 'em?" He stuck his cracked and bleeding feet out from under the blanket. They were cruelly swollen.

"Grandma!" Johnny came in on the run. "We can't get a doctor just yet. Some are coming in from Emmitsburg and around. But old Dr. David Study volunteered for the army and he rode out to the Ridge last night."

"We'll just have to do the best we can for now." Grandma spread a clean towel under the boy's feet. "Mary Lee, you're right handy, honey, you wash out these cuts while I . . ."

The Rebel soldier kept talking all the time his feet were being taken care of. "Ginral Lee's a great man," he said. "He's too good, that's all. Too good.

He should hev told Ewell to go ahead and *take* that Cimetery Hill.

"Sure, they'd fit all day and was tired. But look who's got the Ridge now! The Damyanks! Scuse *me*, ma'am! No offense meant. Ouch! Ewell, he don't like to take the responsibility hisself. But if Stonewall Jackson had been here—he'd have gone on and ended this bloody battle." The boy never stopped.

"I'm for the Union; and I ain't for slavery. But I have to fight for the South. I'm loyal to my state."

Grandma finished binding the boy's feet and rolled him over onto a clean sheet. When he saw the clean bed he began to blubber like a baby. He was a big fellow, too.

Johnny came in with a Union soldier he'd found in a lane, leaning on his shoulder. "I'm glad my leg's broken," the soldier said, grinning. "This is the first time I've had a chance to rest in a clean, real home in I don't know when."

"I think I could set his leg myself, Grandma," Johnny said eagerly. "I saw how the doctors did it yesterday. And remember how I set Collie's leg. It was as straight after as it was before he broke it."

"Do it, son," nodded Grandma. "Mary Lee, you be ready with the splints when it's time to bind him."

When it was all done the soldier lay back smiling.

"Why, I'm in clover," he said. "Ma'am, missy, I've been in filthy prisons for months, lived in a hole in frozen dirt, eaten grub not fit for a hog, almost died of malaria and yellow fever, seen my buddies die—" The soldier fainted quietly.

When they had done what they could for the soldiers in the house, Johnny and Grandpa went up the street to look out from the roof of the Fahnestock Building, the highest roof in town.

"I can't understand why they don't begin the attack," Grandpa kept saying. "It's broad daylight, and Lee was going to begin first thing in the morning. The only shooting so far has been a sprinkling of musket shot. Some sniping around the Ridge."

Mary Lee had gone off to hunt for some iodine in the neighborhood. She came back with a basket full of simple remedies.

"Oh, Grandma," she whispered breathlessly,

"Saint Francis's Academy is full. The soldiers are lying in the pews. They're getting the schoolhouse ready and Miss Lydia Powers asked if I could come back and help.

"All five of the Powers sisters are here, nursing. They've got their own house full too. And the poor wounded men—there aren't enough doctors!"

"Run right along, honey," Grandma looked at her proudly. "You're a right smart help—a good little nurse. And that's what's needed now, more than anything."

Mary Lee hurried back to where the Misses Powers were taking care of the wounded. They tied a big apron around her, and she set to work as nurse's aide.

CHAPTER EIGHT

On Cemetery Hill

Up ON the Fahnestock roof Johnny and Grandpa were gazing toward Cemetery Hill.

"The Rebels are hidden among the woods over on Seminary Ridge," Grandpa focused his field glasses. "But they're moving southward. I can tell. Fighting may start any time now. I wonder why Longstreet hasn't attacked yet."

"Grandpa," Johnny remembered. "He doesn't want to. I heard him say so yesterday."

"Well, mebbe he's smart. They say he's the fightingest man in the Confederate Army. The South outnumbered us yesterday, but they've given us time to bring our boys up now, for sure."

Through the field glasses Johnny could see gray forms crawling through the grass at the foot of Cemetery Hill. Small parties of Confederates were skirmishing around the ridge.

The scouts would dash up close to the Union defenses, drive them back a bit, then retreat quickly. They hid among the trees so that they could not be seen.

"The Rebs are clever at that," Grandpa said. "See what they are doing, Johnny? They are finding out the length and the strength of our lines, without giving away where their own battalions are."

"It's near eleven, and nothing but sniping, though, Grandpa," Johnny put down his spyglass. "Not a cannon fired."

"They're saving it," said Grandpa. There was a glint in his eyes. "Wish I were over there. Blamed if I wouldn't like to do some sniping myself! Johnny, you go on back to the house. I want to watch here awhile and then I'll go down to City Hall. Wait!"

He handed Johnny the field glasses. "Just take note of the position we have. Cemetery Ridge, like the letter U, with the curve toward town. Why, it'd be like storming a castle on a rock. Imagine the battleworks our soldiers have up there. We're ready for 'em!"

When Johnny left Grandpa and reached the

street, he couldn't resist turning south. He hadn't gotten as far as the square when he saw the Rebel pickets on guard. Better go around them to the east, he thought.

He came out on Baltimore Street just as Sammy Wade came riding by on Pierce's pet horse, heading out of town. He remembered that Sammy had been delivering groceries for Pierce's ever since school closed.

"They don't want the Rebs to get the horse," Johnny thought.

But before Sammy reached the end of the lane, two gray sentries rose out of the bushes and stopped him.

They turned Sammy back into town, a gun against his back. They were coming this way. Johnny dropped into the tall grass behind the fence. They made Sammy get off the horse, and in a minute they all went by toward the square. They'd arrested Sammy!

Johnny felt himself getting very mad. Picking on Sam Wade, were they? He crawled through the field, planning to circle around outside any sentries. The field was littered with canteens, knapsacks, clothes. Johnny stood up when he came to the edge of town.

Before him, the Baltimore Turnpike led straight to the cemetery and up over the ridge. It was not more than 1500 feet away. There was some scattered shooting, but—he just had to see what was happening over there on Cemetery Ridge.

If the Rebs could creep through the grass like an Indian, so could he. A blue hat and coat were lying right by the fence. He put them on. The coat was big and hot and heavy, but that didn't matter. A knapsack? No. A canteen, and it was full. Yes, he'd take that.

And that drum and drumsticks over there. He put the strap over his shoulder, swung the drum to his back, stood up and saluted the still air.

"United we stand," he said aloud. "Hurrah for the Union!"

The thick sultry morning had cleared, and a hot sun stood almost overhead. It was maybe a little after eleven. Long, bristling rows of stacked muskets glinted along the crest of Cemetery Ridge. The ugly black of cannon gleamed every twenty feet or so apart.

"United we stand," he said aloud

There was a cheerful hum of talk up and down the lines. The men were bandying jokes back and forth. Some were leaning back smoking, some were boiling coffee in their long-handled tin cups. And some slept on their backs, their peaked hats over their eyes.

There was plenty of coming and going, but everything was in order. It didn't look as if they'd been working and sweating all night. Nor as if they were expecting a great battle to begin almost any minute.

Johnny stood up boldly. He brushed the dirt and grass off his coat, swung the drum around to the left, and came out of the bushes.

"Hey there, you drummer boy! Come here," shouted a sergeant. "What outfit you belong to?"

"This is Reynolds' drum," Johnny said truthfully. "I got left behind. What corps is this?"

"The Second. Where you from? You wouldn't be a Reb, now? And how the mischief did you get past the Rebel scouts sniping around down there?"

"I'm from Gettysburg, and I'm no Reb," replied Johnny.

Half a dozen boys in blue gathered round

him. "How'd you get up the ridge and us not see you?" they demanded.

"The same way they did," replied Johnny.

The soldiers roared with laughter. "Let that learn ye!" shouted one. "He don't talk like any danged Reb."

"All right, boy," grinned the sergeant. "Find your regiment. But keep back of the breastworks,

mind. The First Corps is over yonder on Culp's Hill."

Johnny was close to the cemetery, the highest place on the ridge, except for Round Top at the south end. The Eleventh Corps under General Howard had its batteries set up between the tombstones. They aimed out over the valley. "Will there be a battle today?" everyone was asking.

Soldiers stretched all along the Ridge down to Little Round Top, almost. On the right he found the First Corps, dug in behind the rocks. They had moved the rock fences up from the slopes during the night to build the breastworks higher.

Next to the First was the Twelfth Corps. They were stationed right around the hill and on south, almost to Rock Creek. They'd dug trenches and piled up rail fences and tree trunks for breastworks.

Like Grandpa said, Culp's Hill was almost like a castle on a rock. There was occasional Rebel sniping from below, but the boys in blue didn't even answer it now. Officers rode by, orderlies came and went, on horse, on foot; he could hear them talking.

"The main thing is the reserves in the rear."

Cannon and soldiers, all the way from Round Top along the ridge, around Culp's Hill. And down in the valley, the fields and meadows, the peach orchard where he and the Wade boys had picked peaches last summer.

And now he was right opposite Seminary Ridge, where the Confederate guns were hid behind the trees. What would happen to the Wentzes and the Grahams and the Rogers, living along the Emmitsburg Road?

A quiet hung over the valley. When was this battle going to start? There was a sudden stir along the lines. Soldiers sprang to their posts. Johnny dropped behind a rock.

A whole corps was moving out from Cemetery Ridge on the left. "The Third! It's Sickles. He's leaving his station at the foot of Little Round Top!"

"They'll be massacred. Running right into the enemy's face!"

But it was magnificent. Ten, twelve thousand men, prancing cavalry, colors flying, drums beating, bugles sweet and shrill, batteries lumbering alongside. Down the slope, across the road, across the ripening golden wheat. It made your blood tingle, your heart pound. Someone was cheering. It was Johnny himself.

Down back of the Leisters' house the ambulances came rolling up into place, and stretcher bearers appeared. That was General Meade's headquarters, and Johnny had overheard the men saying there were eight hospitals back of the lines.

A cavalry lieutenant dashed up. "General Gibbons, sir. General Meade's orders: Hold your first division ready to go to General Sickles' aid. No, sir, the general did *not* give the order to advance."

He trotted quickly back to the white house, where headquarters colors flew—blue sabers crossed on a red background.

"A mad move! He'll draw enemy fire."

Suddenly a burst of sound from the enemy's batteries hits the ear like a crack of thunder. Rebel foot soldiers pour down the hills opposite. The artillery fire never stops. But the Union regiments charge on.

"Sickles is pushing them back! Hurrah, hurrah!"

There is a sudden lull. Now the click of ten thousand ramrods pushed down ten thousand musket barrels sounds all along the line of blue.

The valley below is quivering with a dry heat. It is five o'clock of this hot July afternoon. Every soldier is ready for the enemy. Let him charge!

Another burst from the Rebel batteries. But Sickles' infantry fire is giving it back.

Suddenly the gray columns of the Confederate infantry appear on Sickles' left. He is cut off on that side. And where is Longstreet?

Sickles is surrounded on three sides. He is in great peril. He is trying to turn his front. But he cannot. The Rebs are surrounding him!

"And here we sit, not doing a thing to help!" one soldier shouts.

"We can't leave a good position for a bad one, man! We'd be as bad off as Sickles."

"He had to go out, soldier. If he doesn't take the peach orchard and the wheat field and hold 'em, they'll drive him away from the foot of Round Top."

"And what was he ever put down there for?" the men growl.

Johnny could see that the wounded were steadily being brought back in to the hospitals. Hundreds were falling.

CHAPTER NINE

Beyond the Peach Orchard

THE fighting was terrible. The roar and din, the explosion of big cannon balls, never stopped. Along about half-past five, the Confederates came down in a long gray wave from South Seminary Ridge.

As they came within reach of the Union guns, their batteries blazed out all together against the regiments stretched along the Emmitsburg Road. The whole length of Seminary Ridge, clear up to Schultz's Grove, was exploding like four miles of giant firecrackers.

Johnny never took the field glasses from his eyes. The Rebel guns were usually aimed too high for the Ridge; but it looked as if they'd wipe out that whole brigade down on the road. The men were falling like ninepins, and you could hear the cavalry horses neigh and snort.

"It's worse than yesterday!" Johnny cried. "And I'm not helping."

"Give us some drumming, drummer boy," cried an infantryman. "It keeps a man steady."

So up and down behind the line Johnny marched; and the spirited beat lifted their courage. Boom! de-de boom! de-de-boom, de-de-boom, de-de-boom!

Now troops were running out from the Ridge to the aid of General Sickles. Word had gone around that he was wounded. They'd brought him back to the hospital.

Back and forth the battle lines push. Longstreet, yes, that's Longstreet's Corps, they say, is just opposite Round Top. Ewell is opposite Cemetery Hill itself.

"The Rebels are at the foot of Little Round Top! They're in Plum Run Gorge!" The word passes down the line.

"Our boys are behind the boulders. The Rebs will never get out alive!"

Johnny is no longer drumming. Beyond, in the

ripe wheat field, a bitter fight is going on. The yellow wheat is trampled into a flat carpet.

"Here, drummer boy. Hop this horse and ride like the devil himself down the road to headquarters. Hand this note to the general's aide."

Yesterday a message to Lee; today a message to General Meade's headquarters. It looked as though the Union line in the wheat field was lost. A frightful struggle was going on.

The aide seized the message. "We know." He nodded to another officer there. "Hancock's Corps have gone to their rescue."

Back galloped Johnny and delivered the reply. Now, as they watched, the forces of North and

South met in a gallant charge. But these brave soldiers fell before each other by the hundreds. Only half the Union boys who had gone out returned.

The Union troops were being driven back in great disorder. The Rebels followed right up to the slopes of Little Round Top. And now the Pennsylvania Brigade, under General McCandless, charged down the north slopes of Little Round Top and fell upon the enemy with fixed bayonets. A terrible volley of musketry raked the Confederates.

The Rebel forces broke, and fled back to the stone wall east of the wheat field. They were pursued by a line of Blues. "There goes Company K, from good old Adams County," shouted a soldier near Johnny. It was the First Pennsylvania Reserves, and Captain Minnigh, of Gettysburg itself, was leading them.

Johnny felt proud; he tried to pick Minnigh out with his field glasses. But he could only see that there was a fearful hand-to-hand struggle going on down there. And some of the men under

McCandless were fighting in sight of their own homes.

"Hey, drummer boy, you're with the Third, ain't you? Wake up! It's marching out. Get along with it. We've pushed them back beyond the Emmitsburg Road."

And so out Johnny went, a Union drummer boy. The steady beat of his drum made him step high and firm and lift his chin.

"Brrm, brrm, brr-rrm." He kept time with the beat.

A rain of mortar fire raked the field. The regiment dropped flat. Most of them got up and on they went. They broke into a run over the trampled fields. Johnny never stopped drumming.

In the face of dreadful firing they advanced. On the far left, General Meade's men were pushing back the enemy. You could hear the piercing yells of the Rebels even above the scream of bullets.

There was a thunderous roar from behind and overhead. Down sank an entire line of gray-clad men. They lay face down in the peach orchard.

Johnny stumbled and fell. Beneath him lay a

General Meade's men were pushing back the enemy

Graycoat with a wound in his chest. "Our Father . . ." the prayer rose in Johnny's heart. Why must they fight? They were all folks, North and South alike. Only yesterday a big Southerner had saved him.

Now Johnny knew he was dead, for sure. Because he heard music. It was beautiful. It said, "Get up! March on!" The Rebel band was marching right out on the field with their men, marching to music. Johnny stumbled up, but frightened beyond reason he flung off the drum and ran. There was the Roger house just beyond. And the First Massachusetts Regiment, which he had drummed on to victory, was holding the line just beyond the little one-story home.

"Go on inside, boy, and get a drink." The men pushed him along to the door.

In the kitchen Josephine Miller, she was the Rogers' adopted daughter, was baking bread. The warm smell of it made Johnny's stomach almost turn over.

"Why, sonny, you're Jonathan Blayne, aren't you?" Josephine was astonished. "You joined up for Gettysburg? Good for you!"

Johnny nodded dumbly. Josephine was just taking some hot bread and rolls out of the oven. "Here, Johnny," she said. "I guess you haven't eaten all day either, have you?" She handed him two rolls. "Here's a glass of milk. When the bread's cool you can have a slice with butter on it."

Johnny ate and watched Miss Josephine. She was kneading dough, and behind the stove more pans of bread and rolls were rising. Another pan was ready to go into the oven.

"I've been baking since early this morning," Josephine said. "General Carr came by and said there'd be fighting here and I'd better go into town." She laughed. "But I had to finish the baking. And then the soldier boys were so hungry I just baked another batch."

"Got any to spare, miss?" said a voice at the door. "We'd sure relish it."

Miss Josephine stood there in the hot kitchen handing out bread until maybe fifty men had eaten. And the men kept coming. "My flour's plumb given out," she exclaimed at last.

"We'll get you more, ma'am," a young infantry-man offered. "If you'll bake it."

"I'll bake as long as the soldiers are hungry," she gave a pat to the last rolls of dough and set them to rise. "It's a wonder the firing lets them rise."

"Just you wait a bit, miss," the soldier promised. "Sickles' commissary is right back of the Rebel line yonder. We'll just borry some flour. Come on, boys." Six soldiers jumped to their feet and followed him out the door. The firing was letting up. But not a breath of wind was stirring, and smoke hung heavy over the valley.

"You want to build up my fire, Johnny?" asked Josephine. "Tell me what's happened in town.

We could hear all the awful noise yesterday."

For the first time Johnny thought of his folks. Grandma and Grandpa didn't know where he was. Too late to think of that now. His regiment was holding the line on both sides of the house, and here he must stay. Josephine kept handing out hot buttered rolls until the last of them was gone. The soldiers tried to pay her, but she wouldn't take a penny.

Suddenly a terrific roar of batteries opened up. "Oh dear, they're shooting again. Go down in the basement, Johnny," she exclaimed anxiously.

"No, ma'am, Miss Josephine. I'll stay right here with you. Can I build up the fire?"

"I'm afraid those boys who went after the flour will never get through." She had hardly said the words when the six blue-coated soldiers appeared at the door. They had brought three sacks of flour, and a whole sheep.

"We brought raisins and currants, miss." One of them emptied his knapsack on the table. "We're mighty hungry, and much obliged to you."

Into the oven went two legs of mutton, and Josephine measured out the flour for a fresh batch of bread. The firing grew heavier. "You came just in time," she cried, for the fighting roared around the house.

A deafening explosion nearly burst Johnny's eardrums as canister exploded almost overhead. Everyone lay down on the floor, and presently wounded men came crawling up to the door.

"Johnny, help me do for them, until they can get back through the lines to the ambulances." Johnny helped her clean their wounds, bind them. He was getting very good at it, and none were too seriously hurt.

The fighting surged back and forth past the little house for what seemed hours. Then came a sudden lull. The Confederates had been pushed back again.

"The mutton's ready and the bread is browned," cried Josephine.

The hot, juicy slices of meat fell from the knife and were served on the warm bread as fast as she could cut it. "I swan, miss; nothing ever tasted so good!" one soldier cried, wiping his greasy fingers.

And so in the lull of battle they ate, and Johnny did, too. All the while they could hear a furious bombardment going on at Cemetery Hill.

Three soldiers came in, gasping. "Longstreet's hitting the line. Take cover."

"I've got to get back," Johnny cried. "My folks—"

"You can't, bub. Want to be killed?" A soldier pushed Johnny ahead of him down to the cellar. "The Rebs are bivouacking on ground we held this morning."

Miss Josephine was already there, and a dozen men, wounded. The soldier ran back up to fetch another down. A whining bullet caught him and he fell dead.

CHAPTER TEN

Where Is Johnny?

THE Borough of Gettysburg had lived through a long and frightful day. Mary Lee had gone from the Jones house to the church to help Miss Lydia Powers and Miss Mary Powers with the maimed and wounded men brought back from the battle-field.

Mary Lee fetched and carried, fetched and carried, all day. Two doctors had come in from near-by towns. The pews were filled, the benches had become operating tables.

It was so terrible that you no longer were sick at the sight of it, but ran blindly on whatever errands you were bid. Toward sundown, Miss Mary told her, "Go on back to your grandmother, dear."

Grandmother was still busy. More soldiers had been brought in. And some had died, and been taken away. The wounded kept pouring in—by the hundreds.

"Grandma, where is Johnny?" Mary Lee asked.

"With Grandpa," Grandma replied. "I haven't seen either of them, come to think of it, since they went out this morning." She lifted a gray-haired soldier's head and held water to his lips.

"So much to do for these poor folk, I hadn't time to think. They're busy somewhere."

"I know they're helping somewhere, Grandma." Mary Lee was not as calm as she sounded, either. But Grandma was not throwing her apron over her head today.

"Sammy Wade's back," Mary Lee said brightly. "At least, he's with the Pierces in their stone cellar. The Rebs wouldn't let him go when Miss Jennie went to beg them. But Mrs. Wade went to the Southern officer, and she got him to let Sammy go."

"How's Jennie's sister, and the dear little new baby?"

"Fine. Miss Jennie and the boys moved over to their house on Baltimore Street. The baby is five days old and the daddy is away with the Pennsylvanians. But the shooting is bad in the southern part of town."

"Let's have a cup of tea, honey." Grandma led the way to the kitchen and sat down. "I need a cup of tea. Haven't sat down all day. Now you eat this bread and butter and soup I made."

"Grandma, there's something else I heard. You know Henry Wentz? Well, one of the Gettysburg boys from the Seminary Volunteers saw him with the Rebels. Right behind his own father's house, in charge of the firing. His pa was inside all the time, but the family had gone."

"A pity! He was a good boy, too. But he went South, got into business, and joined up there. I expect he was just doing his duty." Grandma sighed.

"I wish the roar of the battle would stop! Oh, how I wish it would stop!" Mary Lee's face was pale. The heat seemed greater than ever.

"It will, come dark, honey. I think we'll have to sleep down in the cellar. It's right cool down there. But I could sleep on my feet!"

"Stay here, Grandma, and get a bit of rest. I'll give the soldiers some of this soup."

When she had fed all who would take it, Mary

She fed soup to all who would take it

Lee went back to the kitchen. Grandma was asleep in the rocking chair. Mary Lee slipped outside to the gate.

She stood there, looking up the street, waiting. She walked down the road finally, looking, looking. Soldiers were still streaming into town. The ambulances rattled by. Where were Johnny and Grandpa?

An ambulance was coming along the Taneytown Road. It stopped at the tracks. She ran up to it. Maybe . . . ? But no, Grandpa wasn't inside. Nor Johnny.

"Who you looking for, little girl?" She saw that the driver was with the Volunteer Corps from town.

"Do you know Grandpa Blayne? Or Jonathan Blayne?"

"Why, sure. You're Johnny's sister, aren't you? The last I saw of him he was drumming a Massachusetts regiment across the field and past the peach orchard. Say, don't be scared, sister. The Rebs were pushed back. We'll have them out of town tonight." The ambulance hurried on with its groaning freight.

The bright summer moon had come up, and the sky was filled with shooting stars. No, they were skyrockets—they were cannon balls and shells, arching over the valley between the ridges, bursting in air.

It was a terribly beautiful sight. Once, two shells met in mid-air and burst with a flash of light.

There were still Rebel soldiers picketing the south half of town. But Mary Lee slipped through the back gardens and fields and came to the edge of the village. She sat on a rail fence and watched the awful splendor.

Fireworks! Like the Fourth of July. Independence Day! The South was fighting for its independence from the North, from the United States. It was all very confusing.

All she knew was that Johnny was out there somewhere. Was he hurt? Lying wounded like the soldiers she'd seen brought in from the battlefields all day? Sometimes stray shots whined overhead. When she heard them she ducked down and lay flat in the ditch.

Suddenly the cannonade stopped. There had

been one last terrific round opposite at the cemetery, and Culp's Hill. But it had stopped! The moon shone with the radiance of early summer. The heavens were beautiful—the earth a place of slaughter.

Mary Lee stole out of the meadow, cut across the fields, and toward the Emmitsburg Road. She must find Johnny. The field was strewn with motionless soldiers. She looked carefully at each face. None was living. And none was Johnny.

She paid no attention to the stray bullets which zinged across the field from time to time. For a long time she searched. Oh, Johnny, where *are* you? Across the valley, almost up to Seminary Ridge. "Missy, some water, please." A boy in blue lay right at her feet.

She held his canteen to his lips. She thought he was dying. Beyond him lay a Southern officer propped against his horse. "Little girl," he whispered. "The stretcher bearers did not see me. I couldn't call them. Could you? They're just yonder."

She looked desperately around. Across the field

A boy in blue lay right at her feet

stretcher bearers moved, hunting for the living among the dead. She ran after them, calling out. They heard at last and came back. They picked up the officer and the boy too, the Federal and the Rebel together.

"What under Heaven are you doing here, missy?"

"My brother," she said. "He's thirteen. I'm looking for him."

She told them what she had heard. "You come back with us, sister. We can't leave you here. He may be home by now. He'll be carried in if he's hurt at all. We haven't found any boy tonight."

They lifted her into the seat beside the driver. And so, crying silently, she drove back into town with them. Now and again the firing of pickets warned them that the enemy were still there.

"Don't cry, sister. You're a brave girl. You've saved two men. We had passed them by."

And perhaps Johnny wouldn't be found out there, either, Mary Lee thought.

"Maybe he's in the Roger house," she said after a bit. "They said he was near there when they saw him this afternoon. I think—he might go there."

117

"That's an idea, sister. We'll be checking all those houses in the line of fire."

The ambulance lumbered slowly into town. They stopped at the Jones house on their way to the schoolhouse, where the emergency hospital had been set up. The stars were wheeling around the sky. It was past midnight.

As Mary Lee got down from the ambulance, Grandpa Blayne came out of the house. She rushed to him and he put his arms around her.

"Mary Lee, honey, where were you, and where is Johnny?"

"Johnny's gone, Grandpa," she sobbed.

"Gone? Where to?"

Mary Lee told him everything.

"Drummin' for the Second Corps, eh?" Grandpa chuckled. "I'd have given a farm to see it! Wait, what you say, honey? He was seen at the peach orchard?"

Mary Lee had begun to cry. "Don't worry, honey. I'll find him. I'm going right back now. You go on in to your grandma. She's waitin' for you."

Grandpa Blayne turned back down the road. There was little time before dawn, and the fighting would begin again then. Maybe he could make it, though, get through the Rebel pickets south of town.

But how was he to find one boy among nearly two hundred thousand men?

CHAPTER ELEVEN

Thunder by Moonlight

ON THAT evening of summer moonlight and the thunder of guns, shot fell all around the little Roger house. Bullets screamed through the air, cannon balls plowed the earth. But the walls of the small shelter stood. And the dirt-floored cellar gave refuge to many.

Soldiers crept in and out. Their wounds were bound, they got food and drink, and returned to their posts. Two Graycoats struggled down the cellar stairs. They were badly hurt. Josephine bound their wounds and stanched their blood.

The rumble of battle grew less. The cannonading stopped soon after dark. By ten o'clock, moonlight flooded the stricken fields. The Rebels held the ground almost to the foot of Cemetery Ridge, and on the far side too, it was said.

"Don't you think I could get through to my folks now, Josephine?" Johnny asked.

"No, no, Johnny!" Josephine cried. "Stay here. You'd be killed trying to cross the road and the fields. The pickets and sentries would get you. Wait till morning. Things may change. This can't go on forever."

Exhausted, they slept. Josephine in her tiny bedroom, Johnny on a folded blanket in the cellar. He woke after a time, the stillness was so great. In the musty dark of the cellar he heard the Rebel soldiers next to him whispering.

"They're making ready naow on Seminary," a Southern accent spoke. "Johnson's not goin' to take this evenin's defeat. I heard his orderly say they'd be gettin' ready two hours before daybreak."

"What's the plan?" came a cautious whisper.

"Brothah, I don't know. Except that Ginral Lee plans to have Longstreet batter Cemetery Hill. Pickett got in last night. Stuart, he came in this afternoon. His men're worn out, his horses in bad shape. But he's to clear the way with his cavalry for Longstreet."

"Well, I cain't walk, I cain't shoot. I'll have to lay here till the ambulance boys come, or I'm daid. But you'd best go now."

The whispering stopped. Johnny could not tell when the soldier left. He waited awhile, dozed, woke, and then crept upstairs. A Confederate sentry stood in the pale moonlight by the gate. Sentries were all around the house.

Presently the eastern sky grew rosy. It would soon be daylight. Josephine Miller came into the kitchen and went to light a fire in the stove.

"Let me, Josephine." Johnny sprang up, grateful not to be alone. He pointed silently to the sentry. "Maybe I could slip through now, before it's too light."

"No, no, Johnny! Don't try. You're tall for your age, and the sentries might shoot. They'd think you were a spy. It wouldn't help any for you to get shot, now would it?"

She set about making breakfast while Johnny built up the fire. Milk, apple sauce, a roll. Josephine began to set more dough to rise. The first rays of the sun came streaming in the front windows as she finished.

As if at a signal, and before Johnny could remember to tell Josephine what he had heard during the night, there came the boom of guns from Cemetery Hill. Thousands of separate musket shots joined together into one great rumbling thunder.

"Another day! When will they stop?" Josephine cried. "You see, Johnny, you'd have been killed if you had tried to leave. But the gunners *are* trying to spare the houses. Both sides have said so.

"Come, build up the fire, like a good fellow. I see I'll have to set still another batch of bread."

Josephine made coffee; she put some of the mutton on rolls, and took them down cellar to the wounded men.

Among them was a young officer in blue. He had fainted from loss of blood when they brought him in. But now he came up the stairs and asked to sit at the bedroom window. Hidden behind a curtain, he watched the field through his glasses.

Johnny watched with him. All morning the furious battle kept on. "How I wish I knew what

was happening on the other side of the ridge!"
muttered the lieutenant.

It was about eleven o'clock, Johnny figured,
when the plain before them became a gray river
of men pouring back across the valley to Seminary
Ridge.

"They've been pushed back," cried the lieutenant. "Ewell has been defeated." He handed Johnny the glasses.

Now Johnny saw the Confederate Army come pelting through the trees. Close after them came the Blues.

"The Rebs are shooting them down!" exclaimed Johnny. "I think the South has some sharpshooters hidden in Bliss's barn. Look, Lieutenant."

"I can't see for the trees," said the young officer. "I'm going to get up into one of those trees behind the house."

"Don't move now," said Josephine behind them. "Here come some more Southern wounded. Stay here; hide in the closet." She closed the door. A half hour passed, and Johnny and the lieutenant listened from the closet.

"General Lee has batteries stationed all along the Ridge," said a sentry. "They have a hundred and fifty heavy guns. I helped place 'em. And back of them is artillery. It will be a terrible attack. They'll sure take Cemetery Ridge this time."

"Looks like we've begun to knock the Yanks out

already," replied another voice. The great guns from Cemetery Ridge had suddenly fallen silent.

Fierce yells rose from outside the house. "We've knocked out their guns. The line is busted! Fall back to Zeigler's Grove."

Again the strange and sudden silence fell upon the Gettysburg battlefield.

"Now!" cried the lieutenant. "I'm going."

"I'm coming too." Johnny ran after him. "I know this country well."

Josephine did not see them. She had gone down to the cellar. They found the tallest tree in the grove behind the house and climbed it.

"The fighting's not over." Johnny pointed north to the Bliss farm. "They're swarming like bees around the house and barn." Suddenly smoke and flame burst from the buildings, and in ten minutes they were a blazing ruin which fell to the ground.

"Look," said the lieutenant, "take the glasses. Do you see some movement over toward the northwest?"

Johnny watched intently. "There," he said in a low voice. "In front of Spangler's Woods. They're

Johnny pointed north to the Bliss farm

coming out of the ravine. They'll come right past this house. And Codori's house, and Wentz's."

They watched for a few moments. Now the gray line appeared through the trees. "They won't start shooting until the men are past the road," said the lieutenant. "Go on back to the house, bub, before that artillery in front starts."

"No, no." Johnny could not take his eyes away. "I want to see what happens. And I want to get back to my folks, I do."

"It's one minute to one," said the lieutenant, taking out his watch. "In a few moments—"

"Boom, boom!" On the stroke of one, two guns spoke out, south of them.

"They're in the peach orchard!" Johnny cried.

"A signal!" exclaimed the lieutenant. "Good heavens, I wonder if that Reb was right, and our own guns *were* destroyed."

Within the minute, the entire length of Seminary Ridge sent out its swift and roaring death. And almost at once the whole Union line blazed back in reply.

"They were just holding fire, letting their guns cool." The lieutenant had to yell into Johnny's ear. "It's like a volcano broken loose." He was awfully excited, then suddenly cautious.

"Don't stir, don't speak," he said close to Johnny's ear. "Skirmishers are coming on in advance of the Confederates. Look." Two soldiers were just beneath them.

Willoughby Run had been terrible, and the battle yesterday in the wheat field and between the Round Tops. But this was more terrible than anything. Johnny put his fingers in his ears, but he could not shut it out.

Buzzing bullets and shells passed between the ridges in a steady stream. From Oak Hill came a strange and frightening noise, some missile that could be heard above all the rest.

It seemed endless, and indeed, two hours of the cannonade passed. Smoke hung so densely over the valley that neither side could see the other. Then suddenly there was no more firing, either from Cemetery Hill or Seminary Ridge.

"The Grays are moving out from Spangler's Woods," whispered Johnny.

"I see flags wigwagging on Little Round Top," said the lieutenant, peering intently through the glasses. "They must be signaling headquarters."

"The Confederates are moving out," Johnny nudged the lieutenant's arm. "It looks like the whole army."

"There must be fifteen or twenty thousand men," whispered the lieutenant in awe, as the gray files came on. "This is it! This is the end!"

CHAPTER TWELVE

Pickett's Charge

JOHNNY felt a great heaviness in his chest. He watched the Union skirmishers fall before the Southern advance. On came the Confederate lines. They passed beyond their own advance artillery.

The Union lines were taking a terrible beating. But as fast as they fell, others sprang up to take their places. And now once more the Union guns spoke out. Both artillery and foot soldiers sent a hail of bullets upon the Confederate advance.

The Southerners fell like cards; and others came up to fill the gaps. Again, and again, and again. They were marching to their death, those men. How many brave fellows would be killed this day? Johnny's thoughts were raging.

Why did this have to happen? Why? Like Grandpa said, there were good people on both

As fast as they fell, others sprang up

sides. What was this fight about states' rights? Maybe folks *should* have the say about the law in their own states.

But the Union was fine. It was strong. You always felt proud when they said, "The United States of America," and saw the flag waving, that flag over there across the bloody field.

"United we stand, divided we fall." And there they were, the Blue and the Gray, falling, falling.

The earth was plowed into furrows. The air trembled with the frightful noise, and Johnny covered his ears. And now in quick succession came one great explosion after another.

"There were fifteen big cannonades; I counted," said the lieutenant. "Our boys on the Ridge haven't moved from behind their rocks. They're waiting until the Rebs get there."

Now the Union guns began to stop firing. Presently they had all stopped. "They can't all be smashed!" cried the lieutenant. "Can they be out of ammunition?"

"Maybe they're just cooling off," said Johnny thoughtfully. "Maybe the gunners drew back the guns after they had fired, and let them cool off."

"Lad, I believe you're right." The lieutenant smiled warmly. "It's not just this battle that's at stake, you see. It's the whole future of this wonderful country of ours. If the North and the South can't agree now, over slavery, and states' rights, and other things, there'll be wars all over the land."

"Look!" Johnny pointed through the leaves. "Now Pickett's infantry is coming out of the woods, and our guns are silent."

The gray-clad columns moved forward. They passed their artillery, their skirmishers. They marched on, in close formation, guns on shoulders, steadily, in perfect step. The red and blue Confederate flag, crisscrossed with the great white stars, rippled above the marching columns.

"Magnificent! And mad!" the lieutenant cried. And the splendor of it took Johnny's breath away.

"Boom, boom-boom-boom!" Eighteen fresh Union guns mowed down the gray battalions.

But on they come. Again and again the Union guns shatter the air, and the gray ranks are cut off like grass. Thousands have fallen. And other thousands spring up. On they go in the face of endless, death-raining bullets.

"Greater courage was never seen!" the lieutenant shouts. "They're marching into the very teeth of our guns!"

Now the Confederate guns speak from Seminary Ridge. They are loaded with canister. The

deadly ball packed with metal scrap clears the road. The Grays are barely four hundred feet from the Union lines.

Pickett's men have reached the foot of the ridge. But a wide gap has opened on the right. Something has gone wrong. But they advance up the slopes in the face of the terrible musket fire—up to the stone wall and the clump of trees.

"They are going on!" Johnny gasps. Tears are streaming down his cheeks. Twenty yards to go! Fifteen yards! Ten yards! Only thirty feet from the men hidden behind the stone ramparts, where Johnny himself was only yesterday.

Now from the Union batteries bursts double canister.

"I can't quite see," cries the lieutenant. "But I think they are storming the stone wall."

Now reinforcements are coming up to help them. They are already at the Emmitsburg Road.

But the post and rail fences stop them a moment.

Now a terrific musketry fire meets them. The whole line sinks to the earth. And another falls.

The Union Army has thrown cavalry and several brigades against the South's reinforcements. The Blues themselves are taking a terrible punishment. Many horses are down also. But they have kept other Southern commanders from coming to the aid of Pickett's men.

The spent, retreating men in gray come limping back. The splendid army is broken, their colors are captured and trailing in the dust. Their officers have fallen. Do any remain?

Nearly fifteen thousand men had marched across that valley of death. And of Pickett's men alone scarcely a thousand staggered back across the fields.

"Which is right, Lieutenant? The North or the South?" Johnny cried.

"The Union, the Union!" The lieutenant was trembling, but his eyes shone. "Without union, this glorious country will be forever torn apart. Don't cry, lad. It's a terrible price to pay. But freedom's worth it, worth—it."

The young lieutenant faltered and put his hand to his breast. It came away with blood upon it. He had hardly felt the stray shot.

He looked surprised and for a moment swayed there in the tree. Johnny seized his arm to hold him. "Remember, lad," he whispered. Slowly he pitched forward out of the branches and fell to the ground.

"Lieutenant, oh, Lieutenant!" Johnny slipped down the trunk of the tree and leaned above his friend. He opened the canteen, tried to give him water.

"He's dead, buddy!" a voice said behind him. "I ought to give you a taste of the same. But for the present I'll just take you along prisoner. Git up! March!"

CHAPTER THIRTEEN

The Battle Is Over

GRANDFATHER BLAYNE was past eighty, yes. But he was straight and lean and tough. What he had seen on Culp's Hill last evening had stirred the old soldier in him.

He had not let his family know that he was going up to Cemetery Ridge at noon yesterday. He hadn't known himself that he meant somehow to go. But in Pierce's store he met a doctor who'd come down from Mummasburg to help. He'd brought extra medical supplies. He must get them out to Dr. Study.

"I'll take them," Grandpa had offered. "I can go under cover of the blue line as far as Spangler's Springs, almost at the foot of Culp's Hill. I was the best Indian scout in Texas. I ain't forgot how. I'll get through."

He had gotten through. And just in time. When he reached Spangler's Springs he found that the Union forces had been drawn back from Culp's Hill. They had left their rifle pits and trenches to go to the aid of the Second Corps to the west, and meet Longstreet's attack.

Grandpa managed to deliver the medicine to Dr. Study. But he had had to wait until the battle had ceased for the night before he'd been able to start home.

Now, as he made his way toward the outskirts of Gettysburg in search of Johnny, he thought, "They were within a hundred and fifty yards of the Baltimore Pike, and they could have taken all our ammunition reserve that was waiting just a little ways below there. If they'd only known it."

He wondered if the North had gotten back all their positions yet. "I'll go around by the springs," he decided. Cautiously he crept through the trees. In the moonlight he saw that a dozen soldiers were drinking, and filling their canteens. Most of them were wounded Confederates. He backed away cautiously and went around a little way. He met a captain in blue, coming down with some canteens.

They had left their trenches to meet Longstreet's attack

Grandpa Blayne pointed. "The Rebs are there."

The captain looked and saw. "Let's get back and report," he said. "We'll have to take the springs back, or the enemy will snipe at any who come down for water."

Grandpa went on up the hill by himself and the moon was low when at last he stood up on Cemetery Hill once more.

"Halt!" A sentry pushed his bayonet against old man Blayne's chest. "Oh, it's you again, Grandpa. You got some more medicine?"

"Nothing this time. I'm looking for my boy. He ran off and joined up; he's thirteen, tall for his age."

"Say!" The sentry relaxed and leaned on his gun. "I saw a boy in a uniform too big for him trottin' by here early yesterday. Said he belonged to the Second. Go on down the road, you'll probably find him."

Grandpa walked quickly down the Taneytown Road. General Meade's headquarters had been moved back because of the firing. Another sentry stopped him. "You again," he grinned. "What do you know?"

"The woods are full of Confederates along Rock Creek. Johnson's Division."

"We know," said the sentry scornfully. "We're going to start firing on 'em from Powers Hill first thing in the morning. What's that, Grandpa?"

"Have you seen my boy?" Grandpa asked.

"No boys around here." The sentry turned away. "Better go down and ask the ambulance men," he added brutally.

"I'll look through the hospitals," Grandpa said.

"Yup, I saw a boy yesterday before noon, walking along inspecting," said a busy orderly. "Cool as you please. He took his drum over to the Second."

Everywhere they had seen Johnny, all right. But only early in the day. Had he never come back then?

"Take a horse, Grandpappy, and go on back there."

Grandpa accepted gratefully and went up and down the ridge. There was no Johnny in the hospitals at least. It was barely an hour till dawn. He lay down with his head on a log to get a little rest.

The bellowing of two big brass guns woke him

at about five-thirty on that morning of July 3d. They were shooting from Wolf's Hill. The Confederates were shot right out of the woods. The woods and all were being shot away. The battle was on for the day.

And the Union wounded poured in. Hour after hour passed amidst the confusion of war behind the lines. The noise was worse here than Grandpa Blayne had ever heard it before. But he was scarcely conscious of that.

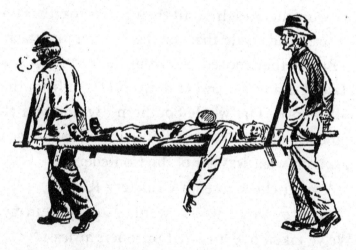

He helped with the stretcher bearers at the hospitals. He peered into every face, wounded or dead. Fear, disappointment, relief, Grandpa felt them all, when none turned out to be Johnny.

"Can you help me, oldtimer?" a doctor asked. It was Doc Study! "Good heavens, man, I'm glad to see you! I'll need all the help I can get!"

The red-flagged hospital tents were full. The shed and barns were full. Red flags marked all relief stations, so that the stretcher bearers could find them readily.

After all, Grandpa hardly noticed the battle. He was too busy helping with the wounded, and looking for a boy of thirteen. It was near eleven when the Confederates drew all their forces together on the east and made that one last desperate attack.

But as they moved out from the east woods, a blast of deadly fire swept down on them from the hills above. The whole Southern division was almost wiped out. Now the Union soldiers charged down on what was left of the Confederates.

A great cheer rose on Cemetery Ridge.

"We've won, we've won! Hurray, hurray. We've taken five hundred prisoners at least."

"It's not over yet! The mad fools! Lee's starting something else over to the west."

When the two signal guns in the peach orchard were heard, Grandpa Blayne went over to the west line with the ambulances. He looked across the plain and saw the Rebel advance begin—the same advance which Johnny watched from the tree in the woods behind the Roger house.

While the artillery duel was sweeping the field, the wounded kept pouring in. The North was losing as badly as the South.

But there was no tow-headed, freckled boy among the injured that Grandpa Blayne could find. One thing gave him hope.

"They didn't find him wounded before," he said to himself. "And Mary Lee and the ambulance orderlies didn't see such a boy among the dead on the field. He didn't come back with what was left of the Second, so he *could* be hiding over there."

The thought comforted him.

When he looked, he could see Wentz's house still standing, and Roger's and Codori's—but where were the Bliss house and barn? Heaven grant that the boy had not gone there to take shelter; for now Grandpa could see through his glasses that the ruins of the Bliss place were still smoking.

The guns had been silent for a space. Now, all

of a sudden, they belched out such a thunder and fire! But the gray army coming across the plain never stopped.

"The stubborn Rebs have courage!" cried the gunners behind the stone wall.

Old man Blayne ran forward to the angle of the wall and stood behind a clump of trees. From there, he saw the charge of General Pickett's men. Never in all his life had he seen anything to equal it.

Right into the very teeth of their enemy they came on, never stopping. They reached the angle of the stone wall. A Confederate general leaped atop the wall, lifted his hat on the point of his sword.

"Give them the cold steel, boys!" he cried.

Leaping on top of a great gun, he attacked the gunner. The man fell dead across his gun, and the Confederate fell mortally wounded beside him.

Two Union generals fell, dead or wounded. But the gunners and the soldiers were somewhat protected by the wall. Their deadly rain of bullets cut down the Southerners the way a scythe cuts weeds.

Off to the left of the Union line, old man Blayne could see the Southern cavalry and foot soldiers too, coming up on the heels of this attack. But they were being pushed back. They'd never be allowed to get here.

Back and back they were pushed, over the Emmitsburg Road. The gallant charge of General Pickett's men stood alone, without support.

The Southern attackers began to retreat from the wall—all who were left. The fire of the Union guns followed them all the way. The pitiful remnant lost still more of their comrades.

And so the last great and supreme effort of the South had lost. The Battle of Gettysburg was over.

CHAPTER FOURTEEN

July 4th, 1863

THE morning after the battle dawned hot and sultry. In the distance occasional shots were heard. But the summer air was no longer torn with the shells and the splitting crack that followed bullets traveling faster than sound.

The Southern army had retreated from the little town of Gettysburg, from the stricken woods and fields. Upon the slopes of Seminary Ridge they, too, were nursing their wounds.

The farmhouses were riddled with shot and countless bullet holes; whole forests were shorn off. Homes and schools, tent hospitals and barns, all were filled with the thousands of wounded. The battle was over; there was relief and rejoicing and sorrow. In one home there was grief, for sweet

Jennie Wade had been killed. In another there was fear—and hope. Jonathan Blayne had not come home.

Grandma Blayne sat with her apron over her head, rocking, rocking.

"I tell you, Ma, the lad's likely been taken prisoner. They'll let him go now, for sure. I went through every hospital last evening, except those to the north, of course, and I'm going out right away again, looking." Grandpa Blayne's voice kind of stuck in his throat.

"Grandpa." Mary Lee was sitting by the front window, watching. She'd never taken her eyes from the street. "If—if Johnny doesn't come back —well, it might have happened right here in town. To any of us.

"Jennie Wade was right here in Gettysburg. A big explosive shell came through the roof of her sister's house. It tore a big hole in the wall and hit her in the back. They said she—she never knew what it was."

"Such a sweet one!" Grandma wiped her eyes with her apron. "Cooking for her sister, looking after her little brothers and the new baby."

"The Union soldiers carried her down into the cellar under the other half of the house," Mary Lee said. "They took the rest of the family and the new baby down through the hole in the wall, too, and they're all staying down there. They're going to bury Jennie in the yard this afternoon or tomorrow."

Grandpa's eyes were moist, but he spoke cheerfully. "Come now, Mary Lee, honey," he said. "You and Grandma fix up something nice, if you can, for supper. We'll have Johnny home tonight, hungry as a hound dog, I'll be bound. I'm going out now. I'll be back come sundown."

But Grandpa was not so confident as he sounded. He went now to John Pierce's store, where he knew he would hear the news.

"You hear about the Wentzes? Wa'al, you know, Henry was in charge of a Confederate battery, and it was posted right back of his pa's house —of all things! He's a lieutenant, no less. The second night he went in to take a look, and there was his father."

"Old man Wentz wouldn't leave, eh?"

"No. And early yesterday Lee moved seventy-five guns up to the peach orchard where Sickles' first line was on the second day. Henry was in charge of the ding-busted battery right back of his pa's own house." Mr. Pierce wiped his brow frequently during the story.

"He must have been scared stiff about his father. He went over last night after the battle was all over, it seems. Old man Wentz was fast asleep. When he woke up this morning—not a scratch on him—there was a message pinned to his lapel. 'Good-by and God bless you,' it said. Old man

Wentz saw all the Rebels were gone out of the fields, and that Lee's army was hustling to leave the Ridge. He never did see Henry."

Grandpa felt comforted some that old man Wentz came out safe and sound by hiding in the cellar. Maybe Johnny had found shelter at the Roger place. Grandpa hurried out and started down Main Street. He met Judge Wills and told him about Johnny.

"No use trying to ride out over the fields," the judge said. "No horse would go past all the dead cavalry. We'll try to help find him, Mr. Blayne."

The valley between the ridges was a frightful scene. Two Union brigades had come down and spent the night on the plain.

"Many poor fellows died out here last night," an officer told Grandpa. "We didn't dare make a light or a sound, though we knew they needed help. The enemy were still sniping from beyond Emmitsburg Road.

"There'll be no burying today, sir," he added, "if that's what you're worried about. And we'll keep watch. We're taking care of the wounded first. The Rebs alone left us near five thousand."

Ambulance wagons and litters were already moving over the fields, hunting for those who still lived. "Better keep your gun handy, oldtimer," they called. "There's likely to be snipers over toward Seminary Ridge still."

Grandpa stooped and picked up a musket; there'd be a cartridge belt somewhere about, no doubt. To his surprise, he found the musket was fully loaded. Why, it had never even been fired! He examined another and still another; they were all the same.

Oh, the poor fellows—mowed down by the guns, too terrified to shoot. Just cannon fodder, just cannon fodder! The old soldier shook his head. But he must hurry.

Maybe little Johnny was one of them. But no; somehow Grandpa Blayne turned away from the scene of death and went on to the Roger house. It was peppered with bullet holes.

Miss Josephine was not there, nor Johnny. No one was there, no one living.

What would the boy do if he had gotten caught in the battle of the second day? First he'd take refuge in the Roger house. But when the Confederates retreated? He'd take to the woods. So reasoned Grandpa, the old soldier.

Grandpa Blayne went toward the woods. He'd search there first, then go on right to the Ridge. There was plenty of movement going on over there yet—the Army of Northern Virginia was clearing out. And what of Johnny? Mebbe he had been taken prisoner again. It had happened once.

And what of Johnny?

When the Confederate skirmisher had taken him prisoner the afternoon before, he had pushed him through the woods at the point of his bayonet. He was a big man and traveled fast. Over fallen trees and branches, over fallen soldiers, Jonathan stumbled, on to Spangler's Woods.

They passed worn and exhausted soldiers, returning from their defeat. Many men limped along, leaning on rifles for crutches. One man staggered under the weight of a saddle, his horse having been shot.

Shells still pursued them, bursting frequently around the fleeing, but the soldiers seemed too tired to care. As he reached the woodland at the foot of the ridge, Johnny saw a familiar gray horse

*He had pushed Johnny through the woods
at the point of his bayonet*

and gray rider come slowly through the trees.

"General Lee!" Johnny exclaimed.

The general stopped to speak to the men, words of encouragement and praise. "All this will come right in the end," he said. "But in the meantime. . . ." Johnny could not catch it all, for his captor pinned him behind a tree. "All good men must hold together now," and the general rode on, alone and unattended, speaking to the disheartened soldiers whom he passed.

In the midst of this terrible and, to them, unexpected defeat, he was kind and calm. Presently Johnny and his captor overtook Lee again. He was talking with one of his colonels, whose face showed his grief.

"This has been a sad day for us, Colonel," said Lee. "But we cannot hope to win all our battles."

He turned then to another officer who came riding up. "Don't be discouraged, General; it was my fault this time—" Johnny's captor pricked his shoulder and pushed him on through the woods.

He slept that night of the third day among the cluster of tents in the orchard behind the Seminary. Johnny was too worn out to think of escape.

The soldier shook him awake in the morning. It was July 4th, Independence Day! The camp was a-bustle with soldiers making ready to leave, and Johnny was chained to a tree. In a hospital tent near by, some wounded soldiers were feebly singing hymns. Many were already loaded in ambulances. Others had gone ahead down the Fairfield Road and some up to the road to Cashtown.

If they carried him along as a prisoner he'd run away. "Oh, no, you won't!" The Confederate eyed him with a hard look, as he saw Johnny gaze desperately about.

"What y'all aimin' to do with that great big ginral you captured?" a Southern voice drawled.

"Just thought I'd get me a little old slave boy to wait on me, like," the skirmisher drawled back.

"Turn him loose!" The Southerner was small and slight, but he had a glare in his eyes.

"Mind your own business!" snarled Johnny's captor. "I can take care of you too." He towered over the slender soldier.

Jonathan was desperate. He could see himself carried away South, and how or when could he ever escape? What actually would have happened would be hard to say, but at this precise moment there was a stir along the line. Through the trees General Lee came riding. Nothing escaped him, as he directed the retreat of his stricken army. He reined in his horse Traveller.

"What is this?" He looked piercingly at the sergeant, and then his eyes rested on Jonathan. Johnny had a moment of fear; the general would recognize him, think he had been spying all this time.

"Where you from, boy?" Lee looked down at the dirty, bedraggled lad in the ill-fitting Union uniform. He did not know Jonathan! Or did he?

"Gettysburg, sir." Johnny looked up appealingly.

"Gettysburg. Why, you're right near home. You'd better get back to your people as fast as you can, soldier." He smiled down at Johnny, and waved him in the direction of the Emmitsburg Road. The chain had somehow disappeared from Johnny's ankle; he was free.

"Oh, thank you, thank you, General Lee!" The relief was so great, Johnny could hardly speak, but his eyes told his gratitude.

The general sat there on Traveller, watching, until Jonathan had disappeared down the hill and through the woods.

Fearful and trembling lest he be stopped, Johnny crouched low behind the bushes along the lane leading to the Roger house. He should have stayed there perhaps, with Miss Josephine.

When he reached the woods he ducked into them. It was right near here where his companion, the lieutenant, had been shot. Johnny ran through the trees, hunting. He wanted to find him. Maybe he wasn't dead—but no, he couldn't be alive. It had begun to rain. The woods were dismal.

There, yonder, that was the tree! Someone else was coming through the woods, someone— strangely familiar.

"Johnny, Jonathan, is it really you?" a voice cried.

"Grandpa! Grandpa! It's me!"

CHAPTER FIFTEEN

Lincoln Comes to Gettysburg

THE hot summer had gone. But autumn had brought no crops. No pumpkins lay among golden sheaves of wheat. The orchards bore no fruit. There were no birds in the trees.

In and around the tiny town of Gettysburg, thousands of men had been left behind to be nursed back to health. Nearly four months had passed since the three-day battle of Gettysburg. But the memory of it would never fade while those who had seen it lived.

All summer, Johnny and everyone else had worked hard, trying to repair the damage done. All summer, the town had been crowded. The Gettysburg folks had opened their houses to sweethearts, wives, mothers, sons, all looking for news of their dear ones. Curiosity seekers had come just to gaze on what they had heard was the bloodiest battle-field in all history.

Now the fields had been cleared. Hundreds of the dead lay together in common graves, the North and the South together. And this October afternoon Grandpa Blayne drove Johnny and Mary Lee down the Taneytown Road to show them where the great fight on Little Round Top had been.

They stood on the rocky summit, amidst the shattered trees. The ground was still strewn with pieces of shrapnel and twisted guns, cannon, and every kind of military supply.

"Just think what it meant to drag the guns right up over the rocks." Grandpa pointed to the great boulders. "This was the strongest fortress of all. We could see 'most everything from here."

"You can see how all the forest is shot away from Spangler's Spring up and down the creek!" exclaimed Johnny.

"I saw a cannon ball as big as a melon in an oak tree at the Sherfys'," said Mary Lee.

"I myself heard General Meade say to the men, 'Men, you must stick by your guns.' That's what did it," Grandpa said, looking out over the plain. "That's why Lee won other battles with fewer men, but lost this one."

"If General Meade had kept shelling Lee's camp, Grandpa, I'd surely have been killed too," Johnny said. "The cavalry did follow after the retreating ambulances. And Grandpa, those poor fellows didn't have a thing to eat, most of them, nor a doctor to care for them, for thirty-six hours."

Grandpa shook his head. "There was no need to do any more shooting at all. The victory was won. The South was defeated. The war may go on for a time, but Gettysburg was a turning point."

Johnny pointed over the valley toward the Roger house. "Grandpa, when we got to the peach orchard, and our men began dropping all around me, I fell to the ground. I was frightened, And then, I heard music—beautiful music. You don't believe me, do you? But that's what lifted me up and made me go on to Josephine's house."

"I do believe you, son," Grandpa came and stepped up on the rock beside Johnny.

"What was it, Johnny, what was it?" Mary Lee asked eagerly.

"I thought it was Heaven at first, and that I'd been killed and didn't know it. But I found it was the Confederate band marching out across the field to help their soldiers. And it helped me," he said wonderingly.

"That must have been beautiful." Mary Lee caught Grandpa's hand. "Let's get away from here, Grandpa. I want to ask you something. One of those Southern soldiers told me that the South had the right to secede from the Union if it wanted to. Is that true?"

"Does the Constitution say so?" Johnny put in as he scrambled down the hill after them.

"No," Grandpa said, "it does not. It doesn't say a word about secession. And all the colonies had to adopt the Constitution if they wanted to stay in the Union. But the South claims the states

reserved the right to secede, when they joined. And that's why we went to war. Not so much because of slavery, but to preserve our Union. When this war is over we won't have slavery, and we will have a great united nation."

They clambered over the rocks in silence, found the farm wagon, and climbed in. Then Grandpa said, "Never forget this, children. The Southern army that fought here was as brave as the world has ever seen. And some of the finest gentlemen, whose like the world shall not see again, fell here. What happened here in Gettysburg was what has happened almost all over the South."

"It was awfully pretty there in the South," said Mary Lee. "I remember Mama when I was little. She had a full, flowery dress. We played with the Negro children. They were sweet."

"And I remember the big houses, with white pillars," said Johnny as they rumbled along the road back to the farm. "And folks were very hospitable, and very polite."

"Well, I don't know what I'd do without you two," said Grandpa cheerfully after a time. "Come spring, Johnny, you can help me get the farm a-growing again. You sure growed up this summer.

"And Mary Lee, you've gotten to be a first-class nurse. And you can cook too, almost as good as your grandma, all by yourself."

Grandma was very excited when they got home. "Judge Wills drove out," she said. "Remember when the Governor came down to Gettysburg after the battle and appointed the judge, as Mayor of Gettysburg, to arrange to buy a burial place for the soldiers?

"Well, now they're going to dedicate it. There will be a wonderful ceremony, Pa. The whole world knows about Gettysburg."

"They say it was the most terrible bombing in all history." Johnny was washing his hands at the sink. "And there were more men killed, wounded, and lost, Doc Study says."

"Well," said Grandpa, "it was strange and terrible in many ways. The army reports they picked up twenty-seven thousand small arms. And at least twenty-five thousand of them were loaded. Some had two loads, some ten. They were never even fired. Some had the balls put in before the powder. And the Confederate powder was sometimes half dirt—no good, they say."

"Well, Judge Wills got enough land, seventeen

acres, for all those who fell in the war," said Grandma. "Come now, let us thank the Lord for this chicken which was left to us."

On a dark day in November—it was Thursday, the 19th—Gettysburg was once more crowded with visitors. Every house in town was full, and Judge Wills was entertaining President Lincoln himself.

All the people of the countryside, people from many states, were there. Mr. Edward Everett, who had been secretary of state, was to make the Memorial address. Generals and admirals, the Ministers of Italy and France, attended. Judge Wills had not invited the President himself until almost the last minute. But Lincoln had accepted.

Judge Wills had written him a wonderful letter, however. Grandpa had seen it. "He said if the President of our nation would come to set apart these grounds to their sacred use, it would kindle a confidence that the dead on this battlefield are not forgotten."

Grandpa, Grandma, Johnny, Mary Lee, and the Wade boys, Sammy and Harry, with little lame Isaac Brinkerhoff, who lived with the Wades, drove out the Taneytown Road once more to Cemetery Hill. A big platform had been built there. The Marine Band from Washington and the Military Band from Baltimore played.

Fifty wounded Union soldiers came down from the York hospital. Their faces were wet with tears as they saw this spot once more. Indeed, everyone was deeply stirred.

The music made you want to cry, and to lift up your head, and to march, all at the same time. But Johnny never took his eyes from Mr. Lincoln.

"There he is! There's Mr. Lincoln! Honest Abe."

Johnny didn't see anything else—the shaggy, splendid head, the sad-eyed face, the tall, tall, gawky body. The prayer and the long and elegant address by Mr. Everett—Johnny dreamed through them.

What would *Mr. Lincoln* say?

Johnny's heart beat fast. He could not understand the prayer which the minister made—"the ruthless foe," "they prepared to cast a chain of slavery around the form of freedom." The minister kept saying such things. But Southern soldiers

". . . That these dead shall not have died in vain—"

were buried here, too, and should be spoken of kindly. Mary Lee nudged Johnny.

"They thought they were right," Mary Lee whispered. "A Rebel soldier I nursed explained it to me. He said the South *was* freeing slaves—many of them. The Southern states just wanted to be independent in government, like the colonies did at first. Right, Johnny?" Mary Lee had a clever way of seeing things.

"Hush!" Grandma laid a finger across her lips. At last! Mr. Lincoln came forward to the edge of the platform. Everyone was very quiet.

His voice was gentle and strong, and somehow it seemed that his words were tender and beautiful. They sank deep into the heart and mind of the boy and of the girl who listened.

Some folks didn't understand. Grandma said afterwards that they were tired. But Johnny's questions were answered. The words of Abraham Lincoln fell like a clear light. Short and quiet and beautiful, they would cast that light down the years. People would always remember.

"Fourscore and seven years ago, our fathers brought forth on this continent a new nation, con-

ceived in liberty, and dedicated to the proposition that all men are created equal.

"Now we are engaged in a great civil war testing whether that nation, or any nation so conceived and so dedicated, can long endure. We are met on a great battlefield of that war. We have come to dedicate a portion of that field as a final resting place for those who here gave their lives that that nation might live. It is altogether fitting and proper that we should do this.

"But, in a larger sense, we cannot dedicate, we cannot consecrate, we cannot hallow this ground. The brave men, living and dead, who struggled here have consecrated it far above our poor power to add or detract. The world will little note nor long remember what we say here, but it can never forget what they did here. It is for us, the living, rather, to be dedicated here to the unfinished work which they who fought here have thus far so nobly advanced. It is rather for us to be here dedicated to the great task remaining before us—that from these honored dead we take increased devotion to that cause for which they gave the last full measure of devotion—that we here highly resolve that these dead shall not have died in vain; that this nation, under God, shall have a new birth of freedom; and that government of the people, by the people, and for the people, shall not perish from the earth."

About the Author

ALIDA SIMS MALKUS was born in New York State and grew up in Michigan. Even as a child she was busy writing stories and putting on plays with the youngsters of the neighborhood. She has always had a deep interest in history and science, and has traveled extensively throughout the United States, Mexico, and South America. Right after she finished WE WERE THERE AT THE BATTLE OF GETTYSBURG, she sailed for England to start research on THE STORY OF WINSTON CHURCHILL. Among her many popular stories for youngsters are THE STORY OF LOUIS PASTEUR and THE STORY OF GOOD QUEEN BESS.

About the Illustrator

LEONARD VOSBURGH was born in Yonkers, New York, and grew up in Plainfield, New Jersey. He went to Pratt Institute and the Art Students League, and studied with such well-known artists as Harvey Dunn and Fritz Eichenberg. Before settling down in New York City, he visited all the states along the Eastern Seaboard. He is kept busy illustrating books for young people, but also finds time to swim, collect antiques, and design and print linoleum blocks.

About the Historical Consultant

EARL SCHENCK MIERS was graduated from Rutgers University and became editor of the University Publications of Rutgers. Later he became director of Rutgers University Press. He has made a life-long study of American history and is considered an authority on both the Revolution and the Civil War. He is the author of many successful books, among the most recent being THE STORY OF THOMAS JEFFERSON, for young people, and GETTYSBURG, for adults.